"Welcome, Miss Hi... he said in that voice... dreamed of, all these months later.

"I'm pleased that we were able to come to an arrangement. As you are already aware, my sister is a handful."

It took her spinning head entirely too long to catch up. To catch on. Because this didn't make sense. Or maybe Beatrice didn't want it to make sense.

But all that shivery heat changed inside her as the penny dropped. It twisted all around, turned cold, then seemed to flood straight through her to hit the hard marble floor.

She understood too many things in that moment.

Almost too much to bear—but one thing above all.

This was Cesare Chiavari. There was no doubt. And he was not only her new employer, he was the man she'd met in Venice. He was the only lover she had ever taken into her body. He was the father of the child she carried.

And she could tell by looking at him, and that vaguely impatient, arrogantly polite expression on his face, that he didn't recognize her at all.

USA TODAY bestselling, RITA® Award–nominated and critically acclaimed author Caitlin Crews has written more than one hundred and thirty books and counting. She has a master's and PhD in English literature, thinks everyone should read more category romance and is always available to discuss her beloved alpha heroes—just ask. She lives in the Pacific Northwest with her comic book–artist husband, is always planning her next trip and will never, ever read all the books in her to-be-read pile. Thank goodness.

Books by Caitlin Crews

Harlequin Presents

Willed to Wed Him
A Secret Heir to Secure His Throne
What Her Sicilian Husband Desires
A Billion-Dollar Heir for Christmas
Wedding Night in the King's Bed

Innocent Stolen Brides

The Desert King's Kidnapped Virgin
The Spaniard's Last-Minute Wife

The Outrageous Accardi Brothers

The Christmas He Claimed the Secretary
The Accidental Accardi Heir

The Teras Wedding Challenge

A Tycoon Too Wild to Wed

Visit the Author Profile page
at Harlequin.com for more titles.

Her Venetian Secret

CAITLIN CREWS

HARLEQUIN
PRESENTS

ISBN-13: 978-1-335-59350-4

Her Venetian Secret

Harlequin Enterprises ULC
22 Adelaide St. West, 41st Floor
Toronto, Ontario M5H 4E3, Canada
www.Harlequin.com

Printed in Lithuania

MIX
Paper | Supporting responsible forestry
FSC® C021394

Her Venetian Secret

Her Venetian Secret

CHAPTER ONE

CHAPTER ONE

No one said no to the fearsome and ruthless Cesare Chiavari and lived to tell about it, according to all the rumors that swirled around the very idea of the man, but Headmistress Beatrice Mary Higginbotham certainly *tried*.

"I'm so sorry," she told his man, who had appeared in her soon-to-be-relinquished offices at the Averell Academy in England, a desperately exclusive and extraordinarily private school for misbehaving heiresses. She was not sorry at all, but she was very good at appearing as if she might be for the benefit of the parents, guardians, and benefactors of the students. "I have no interest in private tutoring."

Or any other kind of tutoring. For anyone, but especially not for the fifteen-year-old in question, Mattea Descoteaux, who had made quite a few names for herself at the school over the past year. All of them uncomplimentary.

It had been Mattea's first year at Averell. Maybe it was not a coincidence that it was Beatrice's last.

As tempting as it was to imagine such a thing,

however, Beatrice knew that it wasn't true. Though there would be some poetic justice in it if it was. She maintained her polite smile and braced herself for the inevitable argument. Because with these great, wealthy men—and their typical representatives, like the one before her now—there was always an argument.

But Cesare Chiavari's man did not argue. He did not attempt to convince her of anything, not with words. He merely sat opposite Beatrice with a pad and a pencil and upon that pad he wrote a number. A rather large number.

Every time she demurred, he added another zero. Then another. And yet another. Until Beatrice was only continuing to murmur that she *really couldn't* to see how far he would go…but he seemed to have no end point.

The result was that Beatrice felt very nearly cowed by the man's complete indifference to the amount of money he was offering.

"Are we in agreement, then?" he asked smoothly when Beatrice could only stare at the parade of zeros, unable to let herself fully grasp how utterly and completely her life would be changed if she simply… accepted.

It wasn't even a particularly difficult job, she reasoned, staring at that absurdity of a number. At all those zeros. Mattea was a uniquely difficult child, but then, they all were. And it was only temporary. Just for the summer. There were no metrics to measure her performance, like exams or reviews or regular slatings by families, guardians, and benefactors who expected nothing less than the total transformation of the young girls whose behavior they'd usually had a hand in crafting. All she needed to do was keep Cesare's troublesome half sister out of trouble, which his man had told her she could broadly define as out of the papers and out of Cesare's way, so he could marry whoever it was he planned to marry in peace.

Behind her desk, she let her hand rest on her belly—the real reason she had resigned from her position. She was still trying to wrestle with all the implications of this completely unexpected pregnancy, but she'd intended to raise the baby on the little bit of money she'd set aside for her own retirement one day. And with a different sort of teaching job, perhaps, one that did not require her—a soon-to-be single mum with no bloke in the picture—to act as any sort of moral authority the way she did here.

But that was a whole lot of *maybes*. How could Beatrice refuse the opportunity to drastically change her child's circumstances, no *maybes* required?

"When do I start?" she asked the billionaire's man, pressing her hand tight against the belly her pencil skirt still hid, but wouldn't for very much longer. One of the snarkier younger girls had called her *a bit hippy* only the other day.

"Mr. Chiavari will be delighted to welcome you to the family estate in Tuscany in two days," his man told her, betraying no particular satisfaction at her acquiescence. Because, she realized then, it had been a foregone conclusion to him. Which he then made clear. "All the details of your transport have been arranged. You need only present yourself at this address in London." He wrote the address in the same sure hand, right there beneath the page of zeros. "You are expected promptly at nine o'clock in the morning with everything you will need for a summer abroad. If you have any questions, please do feel free to reach out to me at any time."

He jotted off numbers for a mobile phone, presumably his, and then ripped off the paper from the pad to slide it to her across the polished surface of her desk. "Mr. Chiavari looks forward to a fruitful relationship."

"Everyone loves a bit of fruit," Beatrice murmured.

And if it hadn't been for that piece of paper, she might have thought she'd imagined the whole thing.

Because it took far less time than she might have imagined to wrap up her life's work at the school that had been the only real job she'd ever had after her teacher training. First as a member of staff, and for the last six years, as headmistress. And still it didn't take that long to say her goodbyes to the staff members she would miss, because she had agreed not to tell any of them the real reason she was leaving. The Board of Directors had been very clear on that point. After all, how could they continue to sell themselves as standard-bearers for moral behavior in

CAITLIN CREWS

11

young women when the headmistress of the school had gone ahead and gotten herself knocked up with no husband in sight?

It didn't matter what year it was in the outside world. It was always medieval on the grounds of the Averell Academy.

"Live by the sword, die by the sword," Beatrice told herself stoutly, as she marched herself off said grounds for the last time. She had set herself up as a paragon of correct behavior. She should have known that it would only be a matter of time before behavior tripped her up, too. Wasn't that the way things worked?

She still didn't understand how this had happened, she thought later that same night in a hotel room in London. She'd cleared out the rooms her role at the Academy had provided for her—meaning she'd put what few belongings she had into a few sad cases and had carried them off with her when she'd left. Now she found herself sitting on her hotel bed, staring at the lot of them.

Beatrice thought that surely a woman in her thirties ought to have more worldly possessions than the contents of three medium-sized suitcases, but she didn't. Her parents had both died when she was young. She'd had no benefactors or caring relatives, and had been raised in care. Everything she'd made of her life since she'd done on her own, with a certain ruthless single-mindedness, until four months ago.

She stretched out on her bed in the tidy room

a short walk from Covent Garden. Tomorrow she would take herself on a bit of a shop for loose, voluminous clothing that could hide her condition throughout the coming months, which she did not expect to be terribly hard. In her experience, no one ever paid that much attention to the staff. And especially not wealthy people like Cesare Chiavari. She didn't have to know him personally to know that. All she needed to do was stay beneath the radar and earn those zeros.

She owed that to the baby she'd never meant to conceive, and now planned to love ferociously and unconditionally forever, no matter how different her life was going to be once the child arrived.

It had all started innocently enough. Beatrice had been one of the chaperones on a trip to Venice with a set of their graduating girls who had distinguished themselves with their excellent behavior and comportment, turning themselves into examples of everything the Academy could do. The trip was their reward. Teachers and students stayed together in one of the grand houses that lined a quiet canal, generously donated to them for the annual trip by a grateful father of an Averell graduate. The girls went on a tour of all Venice had to offer, from art to music to glass to history. And on their last night, after a happy dinner out beneath the stars on a piazza, the girls had gathered in the grand house's sprawling lounge and decreed that it was time to give the headmistress a makeover.

Beatrice had always kept firm boundaries between herself and the girls. It was the only way to maintain order, and she knew it. But on these trips abroad, with the deserving girls who would soon graduate, she allowed herself—and them—some slight bit of leeway. And this year had been a hard one, with Mattea Descoteaux like a troublemaking plague that infected everything. Beatrice had been in a mood for perhaps even more leeway than usual, and so she had allowed them to take down her hair and apply their curling irons and creams and gels with abandon. She'd let them take off the glasses she always wore to paint her face in a way she never had and never would again. She'd even let them cajole her into trying on a completely inappropriate dress in a shocking shade of red.

When she'd looked in the mirror, she'd seen a scandalous stranger.

"Now, miss, you must take the final step," the boldest of the girls had declared, her cheeks red with her own daring. "You must walk out into public like this and see what happens."

"It will be a grand adventure!" one of the more romantic girls sighed.

"I will do no such thing," Beatrice had replied immediately, though she had been smiling. And thinking that really, she could do with a quiet glass of wine where no one knew who she was or had any expectations about what she should *do*. Just an hour or so of anonymity would sort her out far better than any spa, she was sure of it.

"Think of what you told us when we embarked upon our final projects," the first girl had pressed. "Fortune only ever favors the bold."

Beatrice had laughed at that, at the stranger in the mirror with smoky eyes. "Hoist with my own petard," she'd agreed.

And she'd decided it was a gift, this challenge they'd set her. She would take a short walk in the sultry Venice evening on a warm spring night. She could take in the canals, the mystery of this city that seemed built entirely on imagination, and revel in the sheer joy she always felt when she was traveling.

Besides, she'd thought once she'd left the house as commanded, she didn't know a soul in Venice. There was very little chance that anyone would recognize her. And this was a good thing, she assured herself when she caught another glimpse of herself in the window of a shop already closed for the evening. Because she looked nothing like a headmistress.

She turned in a different direction than the one she usually took to lead the girls toward Piazza San Marco. Then she followed her whims, turning this way and that, until she found herself walking toward a little *vineria* up ahead of her, with people spilling out from the brightly lit interior into the walkway.

It looked like no part of the life she knew, and so it felt perfect for this strange version of herself on this odd night. Inside it was bright and loud and happy, and she was shown to a table tucked away in the corner with a boisterous family on one side, and a lone man on the other.

Beatrice had thought about what had happened that night a thousand times, and she liked to imagine that had she been left to her own devices, she would have drunk her glass of wine and nibbled on the little plates of delicacies they'd delivered with it. Then she would have found her way back to resume her life in precisely the same way she had always lived it.

She would have told the girls a story, and maybe even embellished it, secure in the knowledge that nothing much had happened.

That was what she'd *expected* would happen.

But instead, the man at the table beside her turned his head, caught her gaze with his own—the darkest, deepest blue imaginable—and had changed everything.

Beatrice still couldn't believe that it had happened. She'd been so heedless, so reckless—

But even though she liked to castigate herself in that manner, she knew better. It hadn't been like that at all. There had been an electricity between them, so intense that they had both laughed at the impact of it. It had been the way he looked at her, perhaps. Or it was that she was playing the part of a stranger who'd felt no need to restrain herself. She did not attempt to bite back her laughter. She did not deny herself a second glass of wine, or the bites of cheese and honey he offered her from his own fingers.

The stranger in a red dress who she'd been inhabiting that night denied herself nothing.

And when he asked her if she wanted to find a place where they could dance, Headmistress Higginbotham could think of a hundred reasons or more why she should say no, but the stranger she was that night said *yes* instead.

They'd danced in a hot, wild place with bodies pressed in all around, though she had seen only him. They'd danced on the crest of a *ponte* arched above the dark water, and then over it to a *fondamenta* while a street musician played for the quiet canal, weaving his beauty into the night.

Beatrice had felt nothing but magic. It had to have been magic that made her feel beautiful in his arms. So beautiful that when he'd kissed her, she'd melted against him.

So beautiful that when he'd taken her to the private hotel where he was staying, she went easily. Happily.

And she'd tried ever since to tell herself that she had disgraced herself there, rolling around and around in that bed with him.

But even now, when she knew how it all would end, she still couldn't quite bring herself to use that word. She still felt all the same magic every time she thought about the baby she carried.

The child of a man whose name she didn't even know, making her just as bad as all the young women she attempted to mold into ladies with far better manners than she had displayed that night. Far better morals that she could claim, now, as a truly fallen woman in every sense of the term.

And still when she fell asleep that night, the same as every night, she dreamed of Venice.

The next day, Beatrice gathered herself a brand-new wardrobe that made her look round in every way, so that the rounder she became over the summer, the less likely it was anyone would notice. And the following morning she presented herself dutifully at the address she'd been given, and was swept off into a waiting car. She was swiftly driven to an airfield, where a private jet waited to whisk her away to the Chiavari estate, a location so celebrated and well-known that she was sure she'd seen pictures of it many times without even looking.

She knew the man himself by reputation only. Even though the school had been teeming with too many powerful men to name, all of them deeply concerned with the misbehavior of the young women in their care, Cesare Chiavari seemed to hold a special place in that pantheon. Beatrice saw his luxury goods everywhere. The family name was stamped on everything from chocolates to silks to buildings to sports cars. Beatrice possessed the same awareness of that branding that anyone did, by simple dint of being alive, but then Mattea had arrived at the school last fall. She had been hand-delivered by a curt woman who had spouted off her master's instructions and made it clear that he would hold Beatrice personally responsible if the school did not live up to its many promises.

And since Mattea had gone out of her way to make sure that a tremendously difficult feat, Beatrice had spent a lot of time thinking about Cesare Chiavari ever since.

The approach to his estate was spectacular. Rolling hills undulated out beneath the azure sky. Cypress trees marched in rows up this hill and down the next. It was like a perfect postcard of an Italian masterpiece, and this was where she would be spending her summer...

With the most obnoxious fifteen-year-old alive.

Beatrice closed her eyes as the plane went in for its landing. She envisioned a cozy little cottage, on a stretch of beach with the sea *just there*. She imagined gardens filled with bright blooms in summer and a fire inside, keeping her warm when the weather was gray.

She would take all the zeros she would earn this summer and buy herself exactly such a place. She would raise her child there, far away from the concerns of billionaires, and their fifteen-year-old half sisters. She would learn how to cook. She would bake her own bread, the way she only vaguely recalled her own mother had done. She would make her baby the home she had always wished she had while she'd been in care.

All that she needed to do was survive a few short months in a true Tuscan masterpiece.

When the plane set down, she opened her eyes again, and decided that it would only be hard if she let it.

Beatrice decided then and there that she would not let it be anything of the kind.

After all, she had successfully run the Academy for years. She had ushered a great number of young women into the successful futures their families wanted for them. And she was very, very good at the job or she wouldn't have remained employed at Averell as long as she had.

She would not fail to be just as good for a few months with one single, solitary girl, even if it was the provoking Mattea Descoteaux. How could she be anything else?

Beatrice exited the plane feeling a great deal more like herself. Which was to say, she felt like a ball of optimism in steel-toed boots, which is what she'd always told the girls. They'd always groaned in embarrassment, but eventually they'd all usually admitted that it really was the perfect description of Headmistress Higginbotham.

She found herself humming songs from *The Sound of Music* under her breath as she climbed into the waiting SUV that took her down tiny, winding lanes that carved their way through seas of vineyards, armies of cypress trees standing tall to mark the way, and glimpses of red-tiled roofs tucked here and there.

Though even she fell into an awed sort of silence when she saw the house come into view.

It was immediately apparent to her that it was *the* house. *His* house. Because it could be nothing else, and because she recognized it, vaguely, the way she did grand palaces in all sorts of places she'd never been.

The house spread itself out in all directions, claiming the top of one of the rolling hills. The approach was a leisurely drive along the banks of the sparkling blue lake surrounded by groves of olive trees, and it was so immediately charming and picturesque that it only made the house itself look more dramatic in the hills. It was all so pretty it almost hurt.

It was a house built to intimidate, she understood, but it was also stunning work of art.

And for some reason, she thought of that man in Venice. Her lover, as she sometimes liked to think of him, in the privacy of her bed. Because it was such an odd, old word. And because it should have had nothing at all to do with her fastidious life.

But then, perhaps that was why she liked it. It reminded her of a strange woman in a bright red dress, with her hair in a wild, deliberate snarl down to her hips.

The car pulled up before a great grand entrance where two women in starched black uniforms waited, expressionless. The driver of the car got out and opened Beatrice's door, which left her feeling off-balance.

"Thank you," she said as she crawled out with as much dignity as she could muster, not having spent a great deal of time in her life learning how to exit cars elegantly. "There's no need for any fuss. You could drop me off at the servants' entrance."

"The master's orders were clear," said the older of the two women. She had what Beatrice could charitably call the face of a hatchet, and the blade of it was aimed directly in Beatrice's direction.

Beatrice smiled, because she wasn't afraid of a sharp edge.

"Be that as it may," she said, serenely, "this is not the Victorian age. I'm not a gentlewoman fallen on hard times, suspended somewhere good manners cannot quite reach. I'm an educator and quite proud of what I do. I'll need no special treatment here."

The older woman sniffed. Next to her, the younger woman did not have the same control of her facial expressions and when her elder turned and headed toward an entry concealed beneath the grand stair, she broke completely and smiled wide.

"That's taken the wind out of Herself," she confided, her eyes bright. "She has spent days puffing and huffing about who is above the station, and all the rest."

And in the spirit of friendship and the fact she had only just arrived, Beatrice did not take it upon herself to correct the woman's language. Because she had spoken in English, which was clearly not her native tongue.

All she did was smile. "You know precisely what

my station is," she said. "And I would like to remain at that station during my stay."

More than that, she knew a thing or two about grand households like this, having observed them many times during her travels as headmistress, forever meeting donors and future donors where they lived. And often *had lived*, for generations.

Even so, she couldn't manage to wrestle her three sad cases away from the driver, who was now acting like the footman she didn't need. All she could do was follow the older woman who was clearly the housekeeper, trailing after the woman's unflinchingly straight back through into the bowels of the great house.

It was only when they all filed their way up a set of stairs that she began to get glimpses of the house's true splendor. A great hall that rivaled the palazzos they'd toured in Venice. Chandeliers beyond description, with what looked like diamonds hanging in each and every one of them. The space was cavernous, yet elegant, arranged around an open central courtyard that rose up to an intricately frescoed ceiling.

The place was operatic.

The housekeeper continued up the servants' stairs for another flight, but then stepped into one of the house's main halls. There was a library on one side and great terraces on the other, opening up to let in the view that seemed to roll on in pastoral splendor as far as the eye could see. There were sitting rooms, rooms that were filled with art and fine furnishings, and by the time they stopped and the woman threw open the doors of a great suite at the far end, Beatrice was shaking her head.

"This looks very much like the sort of room given to honored guests," she said as she peered inside, taking in the high ceilings and painted shutters flung wide to even more astonishing vistas. Not to mention the eternity pool and a riot of trellises and pagodas.

"You are a guest of the Chiavari family, are you not?" returned the housekeeper in perfectly neutral tones, but her gaze was assessing.

"I'm honored by the suggestion that I rest my head where no doubt kings and queens aplenty rested theirs before me and will again long after I cease to be a memory here," Beatrice said, aware that with each word, the younger woman was grinning all the wider. "Yet for what I am here to do, it would be inappropriate to stay anywhere but in the servants' quarters. Surely we can agree on this."

Once again, the older woman said nothing, but this time Beatrice did not have to look to the younger woman as a barometer to understand that she had passed some sort of test.

She knew she had. It would have been the easiest thing in the world to make noises about knowing her station, only to take the luxurious accommodations offered her.

And it wasn't that Beatrice had anything against luxury. She quite enjoyed it, particularly when it was something she'd earned. She imagined her seaside cottage would be the kind of luxury she loved most.

But today she had far more prosaic concerns. "This is a beautiful suite in a stunning house," she said as she followed the older woman back toward the servants' stairs once more. "I must assume that something so lavishly appointed is closer to the family's rooms. That can only be unsuitable, given my circumstances here this summer."

The older woman stopped, and so Beatrice and the younger maid stopped with her. Then they all exchanged a speaking sort of look.

"Indeed it is," the housekeeper said after a moment or two. She inclined her head down the length of the hall. "Miss Mattea is only two doors down."

Again, they shared a look.

Beatrice inclined her head. "I feel so much better knowing that the rooms you set aside for me can be left open for someone more deserving of such comfort."

And she knew that while she might not have made new friends quite so quickly, she had certainly risen in the estimation of the housekeeper by simply making it clear—without being indiscreet—that she did not wish to be quite so close to her charge. Because no one in her position would...unless they thought such proximity could lead to an elevation of station.

Beatrice had just made it clear to the household staff that she, like them, was here to work. And she let out a sigh of relief when she was settled in one of the rooms beneath the eaves, spare and tidy, with precisely what she needed clean and ready for her. No dramatic reading rooms and such. Nothing more and nothing less than was necessary.

"Why don't you settle in," the housekeeper advised her. "Mr. Chiavari anticipates that you will meet with him when the clock strikes noon. He will be in the main hall at precisely that time. Do you intend to wear a servants' uniform while you're here?"

"I think not," Beatrice said, with very real regret. "I have no wish to distinguish myself in any way, but I suspect that I will need to cling to what little authority I have over my charge. It would be better if she did not think that just because I'm here, she can order me around in a way that I would never permit her to do at the Academy."

"Just so," the older woman said, inclined her head. "I am Mrs. Morse. Please feel free to ask me any questions you might have."

Then, with what seemed to be something terribly close to a click of her heels, she quit the room.

"I think you might have impressed her," the younger girl said in tones of awe. "And she is from England and never impressed. I am Amelia. Mrs. Morse said that I am to show you the threads."

Beatrice blinked. "The ropes, I think. She'd like you to show me the ropes, no?"

"*Sì*...yes, the ropes," Amelia agreed happily. Then she straightened. "But you must not keep the master waiting. It is not done. I will guide you down to the great hall, for it is very easy to get lost. I grew up here and I still do."

And while that did not exactly instill a great deal of confidence in Beatrice regarding Amelia's abilities, she nodded, and when the girl stepped out, she set about freshening up with her usual efficiency. She could admit that she was curious about the master of the house, but the way she was always interested in finding out where her girls came from. Who had raised them and how. The truth was that she was well used to dealing with men like Cesare Chiavari. She'd faced down irate parents from almost every possible high-society echelon in every country around. The only real difference was that she was in this one's ancestral home, where she would be staying for the next few months.

She tended to her hair, scraping it back more firmly into its typical severe bun. She had discovered early on that the more she made herself look like a stereotypical headmistress, the more she was treated as one. She'd been wearing thick glasses only she knew weren't prescription ever since. She blew her hair straight and pinned it up ruthlessly. She had made a study of dowdy clothes, which was why the girls in Venice had been so gleeful that she'd let them dress her up as the very antithesis of herself.

If she could have, she really would have worn the house uniform. It would allow her to disappear into the wallpaper in the eyes of all the well-to-do residents, and it did not take a terrific amount of imagination to understand why that would be a boon to a woman in her position. No one noticed if a servant grew fat or thin. Not in places like this. No one noticed the servants at all.

She merely had to inhabit a space that was somehow a little bit of a headmistress and a servant at once. She needed the authority of one and the built-in invisibility cloak of the other.

But the good news was that she only had to find that particular balancing act for the next few months.

In record time, she cleaned herself up and exited the room to find Amelia waiting as promised. She followed the girl down from the attic, only half listening as she chattered on about this and that, lapsing in and out of Italian as she went.

These grand houses really were museums, Beatrice thought as they walked through the gallery, making their way around the square of it so they could walk down the great Y-shaped stair on the far side. It was the true gallery here, because the light that poured down from above, and a great glass ceiling several floors above them, did not shine too brightly to all the works of art that graced the walls. She was sure that if she walked the length of the gallery, and the floors above, she would find formal portraits of the family, because that was the sort of thing people with money like this always seemed to have on hand. But the paintings she saw on this level of the gallery were not family portraits, historical or otherwise. They were extraordinary. Beatrice didn't have to have a degree in art history to recognize that a great many of them were famous, and others looked as if they ought to be familiar, suggesting that she was in the presence of the Great Masters whether she could identify them or not.

Not quite the same as the sketches and photographs of old headmistresses that had been on the walls of her rooms at Averell, along with the maps of the grounds from different eras that served as her decor.

A bit hushed—she would never say *awed*—she started down the great stair, waved on by a suddenly bashful-looking Amelia.

And as she descended the stairs, the clock that took pride of place there on the landing where the arms of the Y met the stem, began to toll.

She marched down the left arm of the Y, turned, and there he was.

And for a moment, like a small death, everything stopped.

It was like that crowded little wine bar in Venice all over again.

Beatrice looked up, and it was as if they were all alone. There was only his gaze, like a dark blue touch, so intensely did it meet hers. There was only his face, harsh and beautiful at once, intimidating and yet its own kind of art.

She knew. She had tasted it. She had seen the kind of art he made.

And despite the parts of her that were already

melting, and the riot inside her, she couldn't seem to stop herself from taking one step, then the next. She felt her eyes widen. She felt her whole body shiver, and then the heat she recognized too well by now took its place. It wound its way through her. It filled her. It sat heavy in her breasts, between her legs.

If she knew his name it would have been on her lips, like some kind of song of praise.

She didn't understand, but she couldn't stop moving, and still the clock boomed on and on.

It had struck twelve as her foot finally hit the marble floor of the great hall.

And she opened her mouth to speak, but he was looking at her...quizzically, yes.

But not at all intensely the way he had that night.

That was wrong. That didn't make sense—

"Welcome, Miss Higginbotham," he said in that voice that she still dreamed of, all these months later. She had heard it rough in her ear, a rumble against her throat, and as a dark, deep laugh between her legs. "I'm pleased that we were able to come to an arrangement. As you are already aware, my sister is a handful. All I ask is that you maintain an appropriately tight grip on her antics until I am wed."

It took her spinning head entirely too long to catch up. To catch on. Because this didn't make sense. Or maybe Beatrice didn't want it to make sense.

But all that shivery heat changed inside her as the penny dropped. It twisted all around, turned cold, then seemed to flood straight through her to hit the same hard marble floor.

She understood too many things in that moment.

Almost too much to bear—but one thing above all.

This was Cesare Chiavari. There was no doubt. And he was not only her new employer, he was the man she'd met in Venice. He was the only lover she had ever taken into her body. He was the father of the child she carried.

And she could tell by looking at him, and that vaguely impatient, arrogantly polite expression on his face, that he didn't recognize her at all.

CHAPTER TWO

CESARE HAD NEVER met the legendary headmistress of the Averell Academy, because her reputation—and that of the school—had preceded her. After Mattea had been expelled from four schools in one school year, Averell had been the only remaining choice.

That place might as well be a jail! Mattea had protested.

It is Averell or a real jail, Cesare had told her flatly. *Choose carefully.*

And since Mattea had actually remained at Averell for an entire school year, a new record for her, Cesare had not had any need to confer with the headmistress or anyone else about her sins. He had therefore thought about the school only when paying the astronomical tuition fees. If asked, he could not possibly have pulled the woman's visage to mind.

But she certainly looked the part, he thought now. Precisely as a headmistress should. Her hair looked black, scraped back as it was to lie smoothly against her skull and then fastened into a torturous-looking bun on the back of her head that would make even the most hardened ballerina wilt. She wore huge glasses that obscured the better part of her face, and he thought it must be a trick of the light that he was tempted to imagine her skin looked smooth. Supple, even.

He dismissed the bizarre observation as he took in the rest of her. She was not *quite* as dowdy as he had expected, given her profession and the way Mattea had complained about her as if she was the Wicked Witch of the West in all regards. He had expected warts at the very least.

But this woman was significantly younger than he'd assumed she'd be. A fact that should not have sat upon him the way it did, as if it had weight. It did not. Of course it did not.

The only other immediately notable thing about the headmistress was that she was round. And dressed in dark colors, so she resembled nothing so much as an owl.

She eyed him—yes, *owlishly*—and she stood there, somehow looking as if there was steel down her back despite the *roundness*.

She also looked at him directly, unsmilingly, as if she was inspecting him—and finding him wanting.

It was unusual, but he decided he liked that, too. She was exactly what was needed to keep Mattea in line while Cesare was off tending to the tedious, yet necessary business of securing the family legacy.

"And where is your sister?" the woman asked, and something about her tone…got to him, though he could find nothing objectionable about it. Maybe it was her voice itself. It made something in him react.

Cesare told himself it was his hackles rising, and quite rightly, because it had been a long while indeed since he had been spoken to with anything but reverence and respect from someone he had never met before. Someone who worked for him, no less.

He told himself that it was likely good for him to have someone about who did not regard him as something akin to a local god, but it was going to take some getting used to.

Especially when he had a fifteen-year-old sister who handled daily irreverence quite well herself.

"I imagine she is still fast asleep," he said, surprised that it took him a bit of work to keep his tone neutral. As if this was an important negotiation when it was not. He usually didn't bother to meet new staff at all. He left that to the always efficient Mrs. Morse, who had stepped in when the curt former governess responsible for Mattea had quit after delivering her to Averell.

The headmistress gazed back at him in that same steady manner. "And do you have a set of instructions for how her days ought to be ordered?"

"Do I detect judgment?" he could not seem to help but ask.

"Judgment is often assumed, because of my position," she replied smoothly, which he supposed was a nicer way of saying he was imagining things. When Cesare Chiavari was not, as a rule, known for his imaginative flights of fancy. "I reserve my judgment for my charges. Everyone's happier that way, I find."

Yet he felt judged all the same.

He could not account for the fact that this woman had him standing in his own ancestral hall, *feeling things*.

But he thrust that aside. Because it was unaccountable. And because she continued to gaze up at him through those enormous glasses as if she knew exactly what he was trying to pretend he was not feeling.

Cesare could not say he enjoyed the sensation of being *easily read*.

"My sister has a useless father who cares only about himself and a mother who was renowned for her bad decisions," Cesare told her shortly.

"*Your* mother?" she asked. He stared at her, affronted, and she curved her lips, but barely. "You and Mattea shared the same mother, is that correct?"

He suspected she knew perfectly well that it was correct, and more, that she was reading into the fact that he hadn't claimed his mother outright. He could feel a muscle in his jaw flex. "Mattea has been taught to communicate via temper tantrums and questionable behavior. All I can tell you is that she came by these skills…organically."

What he wanted to say was, *She is just like her mother*. But he didn't. And the fact that he had altered something simply to please this woman, or not to *displease* her, appalled him.

"I'm familiar with Mattea's communication style, Mr. Chiavari."

Cesare knew he wasn't imagining the flint in her voice then. It was the way she said his name, as if she'd taken quiet, yet irrevocable, offense to it. He supposed it was possible that she was one of the great many who claimed they were offended at his family's wealth. The simple fact of it. And he supposed he could not blame her. Or anyone else, come to that. Some found it obscene that anyone should have so much, he knew. No matter how tasteful a vast estate was, it was still a vast estate.

Still, he would not have thought that a woman who made her living thanks to the offspring of wealthy people much like himself would have such a reaction.

But how could it be personal? "I do not wish to psychoanalyze my sister unduly," Cesare said in what he hoped were sufficiently quelling tones, "but she did not react well to my announcement that I plan to marry. I expect her to take this as an opportunity to act out all the more."

This time, there was no doubt. The headmistress stiffened, her surprisingly clear hazel gaze going glacial. "Change is always difficult. Whether one is a lonely teenager or not."

He lifted a shoulder. "Left to her own devices she would fill the estate with her friends and throw a party that would raze every bit of it to the ground, dancing all the while in the flames she ignited herself."

The headmistress did not relent. Not one centimeter. "That will not make her less lonely. If it could, it would have done so already. Instead, I imagine such antics have only made her loneliness worse."

Cesare frowned down at the bespectacled creature before him, not sure why he felt almost…jagged inside.

Whatever *that* meant.

"By all means, then," he found himself saying, as if she had challenged him directly. "Let us wake her. If that is what you wish."

He thought that this woman—Headmistress Higginbotham, if ever there was a more unwieldy name—looked at him oddly. Too closely.

As if she could see things in him that no one else could.

Things even he did not know.

If he were a different sort of man, Cesare thought, he might find this woman unnerving.

He did not. What he felt was that *jaggedness* and so he told himself, with great confidence, that it was merely irritation. If it was anything other than that, he did not wish to understand it.

Instead, he inclined his head, and beckoned her to precede him back up the stairs.

But when she did, he thought there was yet more judgment implied in the set of her back as she moved—somehow with obvious umbrage, yet surprisingly lithely, up the steps before him.

None of this made sense and Cesare did not care for things he could not immediately classify. He liked order—it was precisely why his sister, and his mother before her, chose chaos to shriek their endless, torturous *feelings* at him.

But there was nothing chaotic about the little owl with ruffled feathers marching up the stairs before him as if *she* was leading *him* somewhere.

Cesare had no previous experience with a headmistress of any sort, so he doubted very much that he was reacting to the simple *fact* of her and all that authority she was clearly not shy about casting this way and that. Even here, in his own home. He had been sent off to boarding school in England when he was eight and in many ways had been raised by teachers he'd had there, far away in the cold. The rain had seemed to sink into his bones, making him shiver from the inside out.

It had been the making of him, those cold, distant years.

Cesare had much preferred his teachers—good and bad and indifferent—to his elderly father and his flighty mother. He had enjoyed his independence. He had liked the adventure of it, when he was younger. And he had grown to take pride in the fact that he had not been required to depend on anyone, and therefore still did not.

Where other men had weaknesses, Cesare had only strength.

He wished he could teach his sister the same lessons.

Unlike Mattea, Cesare had never fought against

the expectations of his birthright—nor had he used it to take advantage. Even if he might have wished to experiment with that life, there had been no time for the sowing of any oats, wild or otherwise.

His mother had waited for him to achieve his majority before she'd remarried. Not out of any sense of delicacy, of course, but because that was what she'd agreed to when she'd signed the marriage documents that had made her Vittorio Chiavari's wife. Once Cesare was eighteen, she had married with great fanfare, and he had always assumed that she'd stayed with Mattea's father out of fear. That people would blame her if the marriage fell apart. That they would imagine that she was to blame when she preferred to project an image of quiet serenity to the world outside the walls of her home.

He had even told himself that she was not his problem, because that made it easier to watch his mother scrabble for the attention of a man that, even at eighteen, Cesare had considered his inferior.

But what mattered was that never would there ever be any but Chiavari hands on the grand and glorious family legacy.

Cesare had assumed the reins of the family holdings when he was eighteen, some years after his father's death. He'd learned that having been sent away so young made the occasional notion that he'd been abandoned by both of his parents in the space of a handful of years...easier. He had been raised to take care of himself, hadn't he? And he'd had dreams of going to university, but that had not been at all realistic. Not when his mother was not there to help him. It was not the first time he'd sacrificed something for the good of the family legacy, and it would not be the last.

He liked to tell himself that, as with everything else, he had come to his resilience both honestly and young.

Sometimes he thought it was a blessing that Mattea had not had to do the same. Sometimes he thought he almost envied her that innocence she did not know enough to treasure. Perhaps he might have liked to throw a temper tantrum along the way himself, but the difference between him and his rather spoiled sister was that the only person he would have hurt with a tantrum was him. If he had behaved the way she did, he would have proved to all the vultures watching his ascension that he could not handle the task set before him.

He would have made himself a laughingstock.

Cesare had been determined that would never happen, and so it had not.

He had been left to his own devices by his father first, then his mother the moment she legally could leave, and he hadn't had a meltdown. He hadn't flailed about. He had kept any stray feelings he might have had about those things to himself and had made sure the devices he'd been left to were nothing short of stellar.

Then he had dominated, as was his wont.

Now all he needed to do was enact the final part of his duty to his legacy, that being the continuation of it. He had not been avoiding it. Not exactly. It was only that he had decided that he had so many other things to do first. Like build his own, separate fortune, so he need not do anything with the family fortune but grow it.

He had accomplished this masterfully, silencing any vultures who'd imagined they could circle him way back when, and so it was time.

Like it or not, it was time.

And he would not allow himself to deviate from the plans that had been laid out for him, as they were for all Chiavari heirs. His wife would be dutiful and biddable in all things. He would guide her as necessary, so that she could imbue her role with a seriousness his own mother had lacked. Together they would prepare for the next generation of Chiavaris.

Familial duty sorted.

If he was less…invested in that duty than he had been before he'd taken that trip to Venice some months back, well. That was between him and the moon. He would leave it there.

He couldn't comprehend why he was thinking of that night just now.

At the top of the stairs, he moved ahead of the round owl he had hired and led the headmistress and her judgy back around to the entrance to the family wing, where Mattea had been accorded a set of rooms as far away from his as possible.

Once he married, he and his wife would follow long-standing tradition and move into the grand master suite that took over the top floor of this wing. The rooms up there were arranged in the old-fashioned way, with a significant separation between the master and the mistress's bedchambers, so that once the necessary heirs had been produced, the couple could maintain their privacy as they wished.

The mistress's chamber sat directly above the nursery, with its own private stair between them, though Cesare had always seen that as a curiosity more than anything else. He had certainly never seen the slightest evidence of his mother knew it was there. And he had never taken advantage of it himself.

His mother had not been a comfort to him when he was small. And she had been a deliberate thorn in his side when he was older. He did not allow himself to indulge any softer feelings on the subject, much less any *what-ifs*. They changed nothing.

And Cesare tried not to discuss these things in his sister's presence.

"When is the wedding date?" the little owl asked from beside him as they walked down the hall of the lower family rooms, built when families were larger. Or perhaps for parents who had liked each other more than Cesare's ever had, to his memory.

"It will be sometime in August, I assume," he replied.

Though he was struck with the strangest notion

that the woman who now walked beside him, quite as if she imagined herself his equal, ought to have been taller.

It was the oddest sensation. Perhaps it was that air of authority of hers. Perhaps he thought she should be at least as tall as she was round.

She made a sympathetic sound. He discovered he did not believe it. "I understand it's hard to pick a date."

"The date is not the issue." He found himself in the exceedingly unusual position of having to explain himself and did not care for it. "I have yet to propose."

"I see."

He glanced beside him and lifted a brow at the expression that was *not quite* on her face, what little of it he could discern behind the gigantic glasses. "Once again I seem to have earned your judgment, Miss Higginbotham."

"Not at all, Mr. Chiavari." Once again, there was something in the way she said his name. Something very nearly…chiding. He disliked it, but he could hardly continue to insist that her judgment existed when she claimed it did not. It made him look delusional. Or emotional, which was worse. "I was under the impression the wedding was already set."

He gazed at her in amazement. "I do not anticipate that my proposal will be declined."

The very notion was absurd.

"Have you chosen a bride? Or will there be a selection process?"

Her expression was smooth and unreadable, as far as he could tell, and yet he still could not get past the notion that she was making a mockery of him.

Then again, he was unfamiliar with such things. It was entirely possible he was mistaken.

"I appreciate your interest in my personal affairs," he told her in the sort of freezingly polite tone that most people took for the scathing put-down it was. She, naturally, appeared wholly unfazed, so he carried on, from between gritted teeth. "I assure you, I will be well and truly wed by the end of summer. You need not concern yourself with the details. Your one and only concern is keeping my sister entertained enough—or busy enough, or incarcerated enough, I am not picky—that she does not set off one of her typical bombs in the middle of the festivities. Or in the papers before any such festivities. Or at all."

Last summer Mattea had been fourteen. She had crashed a stolen Ferrari into a famous fountain in Rome, then attempted to evade capture on foot, dressed only in what Cesare could euphemistically call a *gesture* toward a yoga ensemble.

He had been forced to decline "modeling offers" on her behalf ever since.

"I don't think she would bother to take the time to set off an actual bomb," the irritating woman beside him replied, almost cheerfully. "So there's that, as a positive."

He stopped with some flourish at the door at the end of the hall, and waved his hand. He did not need to point out the obvious. They could both hear the pounding beat of music—if it could be called music—thundering from within.

This was how Mattea greeted each day and celebrated most every night.

"That is very loud indeed," the headmistress said, but with a little *tsking* sound, as if he was to blame for allowing it. The audacity was breathtaking.

He forced himself not to react. "In my experience, my sister does not play her music unless she is at home, the better to make certain it is annoying as many members of the household as possible."

The headmistress considered this. Or him. Or possibly she was looking at the moldings, so impossible was it to tell with her glasses in the way. "And where is she going when she is not home?"

"In the half week she has been back from school this summer she has attempted to make a break for at least five distant European cities," he said mildly. "With or without the company of the lovesick young men who attempt to gain access to my property. On her own she has stolen, in order, a utility truck used primarily for viticulture, a bicycle belonging to the postman, a delivery van, and the groundskeeper's all-terrain vehicle. She never attempts to leave on foot, of course. She says that would feel like work. In every case, she was apprehended before she left the property."

He did not know how to process the fact that the woman did not seem particularly surprised by any of that. *He* was outraged simply recounting it all.

It had only been *a few days*.

"But it's quite a bit of property, isn't it?" Miss Higginbotham was saying. "You could trek for ages in all directions before you found any hint of civilization."

"A fact of which my sister is well aware, but chooses to ignore." Cesare lifted a shoulder. "Possibly because what she really wants is attention."

"Have you considered giving her that attention, then?"

He stared down at this owl of a woman, who he had employed for less than a day. She was not here because she possessed some vested interest in his sister's well-being. She was here because she was being paid handsomely, and perhaps they both needed to remember that.

"You are to give her that attention, Miss Higginbotham," he told her softly, making no attempt to keep the menace from his voice. "And you are to direct her focus away from me, and the woman I will marry. That is your purpose here. Am I understood?"

"Completely understood," she replied.

And there was nothing impolite or edgy at all in the way she said that. It sounded like a simple statement of fact, nothing more.

There was absolutely no reason that he should

find himself frowning as he walked away, as if she'd taken a swing at him.

And more, landed it.

He left the family wing behind as quickly as he could, not sure why he felt as if he was…escaping a haunting of some kind.

Perhaps it was because he did not, as a rule, spend any time with women like the headmistress. He preferred his women soft and obliging, not sharp. And he liked to see their faces, for God's sake, because he appreciated feminine splendor however he found it.

But he was done with all that. In preparation for his future, he had drawn a line under his usual exploits. If such they could be called. He preferred dependably excellent sex from women who knew that they were in no way candidates for a ring, but now that he planned to take a wife, he had stopped calling them.

In his father's day, there would have been no expectation of fidelity in a marriage like the one he planned to have, but he knew that in this day and age, there were different expectations. At least at first. He was prepared to remain celibate for the remainder of the summer and to sleep only with his wife until they completed their family.

After which he expected that they would come to a different arrangement. One that suited them both.

But even when he had the freedom to indulge his appetite as he pleased, he would steer clear of women who stirred up reactions in him like this little owl did.

Though he had to stop walking at that thought, and shake his head, because surely he was being possessed by some demon to even imagine such a thing was possible. He was not *reacting*. He was Cesare Chiavari. He did not lower himself to the likes of starchy headmistresses who were happy enough to hector their own employers.

The very idea was absurd.

He forced himself to think instead of the lovely Marielle, the meek and proper heiress he had determined would be perfect for the role of his wife. It had been no easy selection.

The mother of his heirs had to be pure. Untouched. She should exude virtue, not because of any ancient stipulation in that regard, but because Cesare's own mother had fallen short in that regard. Vittorio had been so charmed by her beauty, and the presence she'd brought to her roles in the cinema that had made her a household name in Italy, that he had thrown all caution to the wind.

But he had never trusted her. Ever.

The actress he had become obsessed with became a wife Vittorio had watched over jealously. Angrily. Convinced that every man she encountered was her lover.

Until, according to all reports, she decided that if she was already to be accused of the crime, she might as well commit it.

And thus she had.

Cesare did not intend to make his father's same mistakes. He would choose a woman who was appropriate, not one who set his blood afire.

He had always avoided the very hints of such elements. He had watched his father suffer, and his mother too, and he wanted no such affliction.

When he and his wife decided, as coolheaded and thoughtful adults, that they might prefer other partners, there would be no jealousy. They would conduct themselves discreetly. They would keep in mind, always, that their children did not need to know the contours of their relationship.

Dynastic marriage was by necessity a business arrangement, and Cesare wanted no talk of love or emotion or unpleasant feelings to pollute his. He would regard his wife well. He hoped for the same in return.

He wanted no part of any *hauntings*. He did not wish to sit around in his own office, in his own house, puzzling over the behavior of a woman he hardly knew and did not wish to know any better.

He spent enough time doing exactly that over his sister's antics. But Mattea was fifteen. He intended to stamp out her behavior and when he did, he would make certain there were no more disruptions in his life.

There would be peace. Continued prosperity. And

the perfection he had prided himself on since he was eighteen.

He just needed the surprisingly disconcerting Miss Higginbotham to do her damned job.

CHAPTER THREE

BEATRICE STOOD STILL outside Mattea's room for a long time. Much longer than necessary. If there had been anyone there to see her, she never would have allowed herself to *linger* like this, because it was a clear sign that she'd been thrown for a significant loop and normally she made certain to present herself as completely and totally unflappable.

But this situation was…beyond her.

She was frozen into place, grateful that the music from behind the door was so loud. It drowned out her own too-fast breathing, so while she could *feel* the way her pulse pounded and she could *feel* the way the little air in her lungs sawed in and out, she couldn't *hear* it.

It seemed a blessing and she was in dire need.

She didn't know how she'd managed to…have a conversation with him. To talk to him the way he was talking to her, as if they had never met.

At first she'd wondered if he was playing some kind of game. Had he hunted her down and lured her here? Her heart had leaped at the notion—but he hadn't broken. He hadn't called her *cara*, the way he had in Venice.

She still couldn't quite believe that he didn't recognize her. Was she really *that* altered in appearance? It wasn't as if she was wearing a costume. But she'd given him the benefit of the doubt. If he hadn't engineered her coming to Italy *because* of their night together, it made sense that he wouldn't expect to see the woman from that night in his home today. And she knew full well that no one saw *her* when they looked at her. They saw the headmistress. They saw the school.

That had always been the only thing she wanted them to see.

Still, she'd waited for him to recognize her anyway. Her voice. The color of her eyes. *Her.* But as the conversation went on and he didn't seem to catch on, it became hideously clear to her that he really, truly didn't know who she was.

And though Beatrice was certain that she would have recognized him anywhere and at any time, even if she was blind and deaf, she started to realize that it would be far worse if he *did* recognize her now.

That he would likely think that *she* had somehow contrived to meet him here, to track him down in this house that would never have admitted her otherwise. That he was the sort if man who would assume that anyone with less wealth than him—meaning, most people alive in the world—would by definition wish to seek him out to exploit whatever connection they could claim with him.

The idea that he would look at her and see some kind of *gold digger* made her skin go clammy.

And now here she was. Neck-deep in a mess she didn't know how to get out of—and never would have gotten into if she'd had any idea who he was.

She had realized, too late, that she'd assumed she knew what he looked like because she'd heard his name so often.

Perhaps you should make a note to look these things up, she told herself acidly. *Should you find yourself in this position again.*

The idea of this happening *again* made her think she might actually break out in hysterical laughter, but she held it at bay. She tried to get her breathing back under control. She tried to *think*.

Because she needed to find a solution to this…but none came to mind.

Beatrice had found the father of her child. But instead of celebrating that the way she wanted to— the way she'd imagined she would if she ever came upon him, the way she'd hoped she would one day— she had discovered that he didn't know her when he saw her.

That she was that unmemorable. Or perhaps it was simply that he had such nights all the time, so why would theirs stand out—though *that* thought made her want to do something truly out of character. Like scream to drown out the music.

Or cry.

And that was because of the situation on its own. That wasn't even getting into the fact he had just discussed his upcoming nuptials to a lucky bride he had yet to propose to with her.

The lucky bride that he had yet to *select*.

She hated that she knew anything about this. Or him. She preferred the man he'd been in her head since Venice. That mysterious, miracle of a man who had come from nowhere, given her the best night of her life, and left her changed forever.

The man who had claimed he was not passionate, but had showed her nothing but.

She wasn't prepared to let go of that version of him. But she had no choice, did she? Particularly since *this* version of him seemed about as passionate as a glacier.

Beatrice urged herself to buck up and carry on, but instead she stayed where she was. Reeling around and around inside her head while Mattea's obnoxious music pounded on and on and on.

For the first time in as long as she could remember, Beatrice wanted nothing so much as to turn and run.

Away from this place. Away from a man who could have turned her inside out the way he had…and yet not know who she was when he saw her again. Away from the possibility, now that she hadn't introduced herself, that he would discover that he knew her—and that she was pregnant with his baby—and wreck her life once again.

"A person could argue that it's the smart thing to do," she muttered to herself. "To run away from here before that can happen."

But she didn't make a move. She didn't march for the servants' quarters, grab her cases, and ask Mrs. Morse to provide her with a ride to the nearest village so she could make her own travel arrangements. She wanted to. Oh, how she wanted to. She could perfectly visualize every step she needed to take…

Yet she didn't walk back down the hallway to begin the process of leaving this mess behind her.

Beatrice Mary Higginbotham did not run away from her problems. She solved them.

She stood straighter, there outside Mattea's loud door. She squared her shoulders and forced herself to breathe, slow and deep, the way she advised the girls to do when they felt otherwise moved to shout and carry on.

What she absolutely did not do was give in to the deeply uncharacteristic urge to simply…collapse. And curl herself up on the floor where she could weep and weep and weep.

Because whether she liked it or not, her feelings had nothing to do with this. It was just as well she'd learned that today. Before she'd had time to really settle in here and imagine that things were different.

The truth was that she had nursed some romantic notions about the father of her child. She'd assumed that after the child was born she would return to Venice and seek him out, if it was at all possible. That was the thing she hadn't dared to admit to herself even last night, lying in that tiny hotel room, thinking of the night they'd shared.

It had always been her intention to do her best to find her child's father and see if what had bloomed between them that night was worth pursuing. If it was still there at all.

Now she knew that by the time she found him, if she'd been able to find him, he would have already been married. So this was a gift, it really was, to discover that he was the kind of man who could look at a woman he had tasted as thoroughly as he had tasted her and not recognize her at all.

And though there was still something in her that urged her to run, she tamped it down as ruthlessly as she could.

Because all the practical considerations that had brought her here were precisely the same, recognition or no. She had already expected her months here in Italy to be difficult, because Mattea was difficult and because she needed to hide her pregnancy while she handled the girl. She had expected her personal feelings to involve exhaustion and exasperation, nothing more.

But no matter what she felt, it was still only a summer. A few short months. Not very long at all.

How could she possibly do anything but stay? Surely she owed her child what this summer promised to deliver, if nothing else. If she couldn't give her baby its father, she would give it the next best thing: a life without financial insecurity built on the foundation of her father's money.

It was more than most women in her position had, and she knew it.

Armed with what felt like the first weapon she'd managed to wield since she'd walked down that stair and laid eyes upon the last man she'd expected to see today, Beatrice knocked sharply at the door. She waited, not surprised when there was no answer from within, then knocked again.

When there was only the same pounding music and nothing else, she opened the door and walked inside.

If she'd thought about it, she would have understood that she would not be walking into a dormitory room like the ones the girls lived in at school. Obviously. The Averell dormitories boasted far nicer rooms than any she'd lived in when she was the same age, despite the many complaints from the usual pampered inmates.

Even so, it took her moments to process that Mattea's rooms were even more spectacular than the guest rooms she'd been shown earlier. She had to find her way through a rabbit warren of interconnected chambers, salons, an indoor hot tub and sauna, what looked like three separate libraries, and an expansive media center. All to find her way to the actual bedchamber, where Beatrice was not in the least surprised to find the notorious Mattea Descoteaux herself.

The girl was a sullen lump beneath a mound of linens in the center of the high, canopied bed, though she was clearly not asleep. She had her knees up and her mobile in her hand, and she did not appear to notice that she was no longer alone.

How could she, in the midst of this racket?

Beatrice looked around for the speakers responsible for the clamor and found them quickly. There were only two of the tiny ones the kids used these days, tossed haphazardly on the polished surfaces of ancient antiques with a thoughtlessness that could only be achieved by someone who had never spent even a moment of her life considering the actual cost of things. Much less the whole of her adolescence.

Not that Beatrice could begrudge her for that. She would not wish the kind of childhood *she'd* had on anyone, and she'd been lucky enough in the care homes she'd lived in. Far luckier than some.

Nonetheless, the automatic calculations she did whenever she saw anything dear kicked in whether she liked it or not. And it was going to make her dizzy if she kept doing it here. It was like sitting across from Cesare Chiavari's man again, watching zeros fill his pad. She gathered up the speakers, found the buttons to power them down, and did so.

And when the room was suddenly, glaringly silent, she waited. She stayed where she was, watching the mound in the bed.

Mattea groaned as if attacked. She sat up in a rush of drama and irritation—

Then caught sight of Beatrice.

For a moment, the two of them did nothing but gaze at each other.

Like so many of her students—former students, Beatrice corrected herself—Mattea had been gifted with a significant amount of genetic privilege to go hand in hand with the fortune she was likely to burn through before she was thirty. Where her half brother was dark and brooding, Mattea had the face of a celestial choir girl. Cheeks like a cherub with a sulky mouth and eyes the limpid blue of the lake just outside the windows.

She used her angelic looks to her advantage, always. She had not liked that Beatrice was unaffected.

"I knew that I was stuck in a never-ending nightmare already," Mattea said, in that cultured, accented English she used that made her seem interesting even to the girls at Averell who shared her background. "Wait, though. Is this a bad trip? Or no, it's worse than that, isn't it? I've actually died and gone to hell."

"It's a delight to see you again too, Miss Descoteaux," Beatrice replied smoothly.

And it felt like another gift, to slide so easily back into this role she knew so well. It was easy to sound arch and frigid at once. It was easy to take on all her headmistress attributes, as if they were simply another part of her instead of a role she'd taught herself how to play.

When she was playing headmistress, a voice inside her pointed out, there was no room for personal feelings. There was no possibility of any crumpling to the ground and weeping like an opera heroine. There was only her authority and the way she wielded it.

She smiled at the girl. "Am I to understand that you were not made aware that I would be joining you for the summer?"

"Who would make me aware of something so horrific?" Mattea replied, her voice shifting over into that sulky sort of drawl she used when she was of a mind to be the most provoking. "No one would dare."

Beatrice made as if to consider that a moment, then smiled a bit more pointedly. "I wonder if that is because you treat your family and the staff here to the same outrageous and unacceptable behavior that we were at great pains to do away with over the school year."

Mattea scowled and even then she looked almost cute instead of sulky and insolent. It was one of her superpowers.

Luckily it had long since ceased to work on Beatrice. In truth it never had.

"I thought you quit," she said, her expression clearing when Beatrice did nothing but gaze back at her. "Everyone said you did. Obviously, that was the best news anyone had received in ages. A great many parties have been planned for next term, let me tell you."

"It is true that I am no longer headmistress of

the Averell Academy," Beatrice confirmed. Mildly. "But too many celebrations on your part would, I fear, be premature. Your brother has hired me for the summer. I am to be your constant companion, Miss Descoteaux. Are you not filled with joy at the prospect? I know I am."

She watched the girl closely. The way she flared her nostrils as if trying not to react while color flooded her cheeks. The way her eyes widened as if she felt betrayed.

Beatrice felt a pang for her, because she knew too well what it was like to have her life forever in the hands of others. She wanted to sympathize, but knew Mattea would not accept it. Not from her.

But what she was really looking for came next, when Mattea pulled in a dangerously deep breath.

"If you begin to scream bloody murder, as I know you love to do," Beatrice told her quietly, "you won't like the consequences. Allow me to promise you that straight off."

"We're not in that jail you call a school anymore," Mattea threw right back. "You can't possibly believe that you're going to get away with treating me like anything but what I am. A member of the family. And if you work here, I'm your boss."

"Your brother is my boss, child," Beatrice said, with a laugh. "And do you know what he hired me to do?" She didn't wait for Mattea to offer suggestions, though she was sure they would all be creative. "All he asks me is that I keep you under control. Now ask yourself this. Do you truly think that he cares how I do it?"

Mattea's cheeks grew brighter, and her sense of injury was like a living thing in the room between them. "If I complain..." she began.

"I imagine you complain loud, often, and long." Beatrice raised her brows. "What have those complaints achieved, do you think?"

She already knew the answer. She knew, very well, the profile of the girls whose families sent them to a school like Averell. Sometimes they truly were dangers to themselves and others, but usually that was something that could be addressed with the proper counseling that their relatives preferred to pretend no one in their august bloodlines required.

More often, the girls were simply lost, like Mattea. Desperate for the attention of the very people who had not only stopped giving them any, but had sent them off to a place like Averell so that they could not be bothered with the behaviors they had likely helped encourage.

It was another reason to be glad Cesare had not recognized her. Beatrice liked people who helped others instead of throwing money at problems and expecting everyone else to clean up the mess.

That was what she couldn't help but think while Mattea sat there in her bed, looking much too young and as if, once again, a rug had been torn out from under her. This was what Beatrice had reminded the other teachers at the school. When Mattea tried to sneak off the school grounds, taking entirely too many of her classmates with her in the vehicle she'd stolen. When Mattea had broken the House Rules every single day for a month and laughed when given the usual chores as punishment, doing her best to encourage a rebellion in the other students. When Mattea had dyed the hair of every first-year purple, green, and pink the day before the term ended and all the girls were headed home for Christmas with their disapproving families.

During each of these disasters, Beatrice had reminded everyone that, while maddening, Mattea was still a kid. More than that, she was a kid who had lived through a lot of loss in her life. The death of her mother. The loss of her father, who had surrendered his parental rights. Her only family was her brother, now her guardian, who was clearly too busy to deal with her.

And was now in a rush to marry and no doubt produce perfect little children who would not behave the way Mattea did.

No wonder the girl thought she had no course of action but to misbehave.

"This is not something I would say at the school, were we there," Beatrice told her, because she always thought that the girls who came to her were talked down to quite enough. She leveled with them, like it or not. Mattea was too aware of her place in the world and yet had no power whatsoever. Beatrice could relate to that.

"Is this where you think we're going to become best friends?" the teenager asked, with scathing disdain. "Because thank you, I'm good."

If Beatrice could be deterred by teenage contempt, she would not have made it through her first day as a teacher, long ago. "I know you like to imagine that I take some pleasure in crushing young girls' wills, Miss Descoteaux, but you could not be more mistaken. My goal has only and ever been to teach young women how best to use the tools they have to claim their own power and whatever roles they might find themselves inhabiting."

She lifted a hand when Mattea started to argue. "Negative attention is not power. It leads to this. To my being hired to deal with you for the summer instead of allowing you to do things that you might like to do on your own."

"You could let me do what I like," Mattea offered, but not as if she thought Beatrice might.

"No one can trust you to behave in a manner that would allow you independence," Beatrice said, not unkindly, though she saw the girl hide a wince anyway. "And only you can change that."

"That sounds like a great laugh. Cheers."

Mattea was looking away then, as if bored. Beatrice pushed on. "I won't be surprised at all if you feel you must test me, likely as soon as possible, to see if I really intend to maintain the sort of order here that I did at the school. I can tell you now that I do intend exactly that. And when you decide to push at those boundaries, remember this. You have yet to set me a test I did not pass, Mattea. If I were you, I would learn from that."

Beatrice waited for a moment, watching the color deepen in Mattea's cheeks and wash all over her face. She didn't point out that she could see it or that she knew it meant there was a war going on inside the girl. What she did was incline her head as if they'd come to an agreement. "The first thing we will be instituting are reasonable hours, many of them quiet. Regular meals, regular exercise, no subjecting the whole of Tuscany to your music. This is nonnegotiable."

"I don't get up before noon and I don't *exercise*," Mattea shot back, the temper making her flush then, the way it always did. Beatrice assumed it felt better than the misery. "You can't make me."

Beatrice saw no need to argue about that. Not yet. "You look out of sorts, Mattea," she said instead. "As if you stayed up too late, slept terribly, and are in dire need of sustenance. If you looked happy, strong, and well rested, it wouldn't matter what hours you kept or how you cared for yourself."

"You should do something about your weird obsession with other people's lives," the girl told her, with a sneer.

"Prove to me that you can care for yourself," Beatrice said gently, "and I will not feel the need to impose care upon you."

This time, Mattea looked something like ashamed,

and clearly hated that she did. Because she immediately flung herself backward into her bed and pulled the covers up over her. "Go away," came her muffled voice.

"You have an hour," Beatrice told her. "I would like you to rise, shower, and dress yourself in something appropriate for walking. I will need a tour of the house and grounds and would like you to give it to me. That is how you and I will spend our first day together. And no," she said as the mound of covers shook with obvious outrage, "I will not go off and wait for you somewhere else in this rambling mansion so you can pretend you can't find me. I'll be right here."

The covers moved slightly, so Mattea could peer out at her.

And Beatrice said nothing further. She didn't need to. She didn't need to threaten the girl or list out the consequences Mattea might face if she refused. She knew that Mattea was running through all the times Beatrice had been as good as her word—that being every time. And all the times Mattea had bested her—that being none.

They stayed like that, locked in a silent battle of wills, for a long time.

So long that Beatrice had to remind herself that at the end of the day, what Mattea liked most was attention. And she had proved extremely interested in getting Beatrice's over the course of this last year.

Besides, she was fifteen, very pampered, and thought she was far tougher than she was.

All Beatrice had to do was maintain her cool and refuse to break.

And sure enough, Mattea eventually let out a theatrical groan. She threw the covers back and stormed up and out of the bed. She muttered things that Beatrice did her a favor by pretending not to hear while she stomped into the adjoining bathroom suite and slammed the door.

Beatrice, true to her word, did not quit the bedroom. When she didn't hear the water go on inside the bathroom, she went and knocked on the door. "Do you need help turning on the water?" she called.

And smiled when she heard a clattering sound that she suspected was a mobile tossed with some force onto a counter. Then something that sounded suspiciously like a scream of rage before she finally heard the sound of water.

She went over to look out Mattea's windows and was struck once again by the sheer, unimaginable beauty of this place. Mattea's rooms looked out over a perfectly maintained garden, with summer flowers in full bloom. The hills in the distance were covered in neat rows of vines. Beatrice thought it must be possible to stand here for an eternity and never get sick of the view.

But thinking such things was dangerous, because it led her back to thinking of Cesare.

Something she was going to have to learn how

to do without giving herself away. She had the urge to slide her hands down over that thickening at her belly that had become a kind of touchstone, but she didn't. Because that was giving herself away too and she had to break herself of the habit.

Because nothing mattered more than her child's future. She needed to keep that at front of mind.

Mattea eventually emerged from the bathroom naked, looking for a reaction she didn't get. She dressed languidly, then condescended to take Beatrice all around the house, the gardens, and a little swath of the vineyards. By the time they were done, she was wilting about, claiming that she was starving. Beatrice conferred with Amelia and had a proper tea brought up to one of Mattea's salons.

And she noticed that like most children and all puppies, Mattea was far more biddable when she wasn't hungry. Once she filled her belly, she stopped trying to prove how bad to the bone she was and was actually rather polite, automatically.

"You've gone to such lengths to convince us all you have no manners," Beatrice pointed out after this went on through a second round of perfectly toasted crumpets. "Apparently that, too, is an act."

The teenager sniffed. "Your whole thing is an act. I bet you don't even look fussy like that when you're alone. *I* don't run around in a costume."

One thing Beatrice knew about kids is that they were often frighteningly accurate.

She didn't react. "The difference is that 'my whole thing,' as you put it, is a job."

"Whatever you need to believe." Mattea shrugged, and then set down the last of the crumpet she'd been eating, dripping with jam and butter. "I know what Cesare thinks, but my mother wasn't the waste of space he pretends. She just didn't like being alone." A vulnerable expression moved over her face but she seemed to realize it, so she blinked and looked down at her lap. "She liked pretty things and delicate behavior, so she taught me both, but not because she was all that fragile. But because the more people thought of her as breakable, the better they treated her."

And there were so many questions that Beatrice wanted to ask at that. About her mother. About Cesare. About whether or not Mattea considered herself breakable, or why she went out of her way not to use the pretty, delicate behavior her mother had taught her—

But the girl stood up, pushing away from the table as if she'd suddenly remembered that she ought to have been in a fury this whole time. "He hired you to be my babysitter because you're the only headmistress who didn't kick me out of school within a month. But that just means that I'm better at manipulating you than the others, doesn't it?"

"That's one story," Beatrice said, with a smile. "Is that what you tell yourself?"

"Anyway, it doesn't matter." Mattea huffed out a

sound that managed to convey her bone-deep disgust in all things, but especially Beatrice. "The thing about Cesare is that he thinks I'm an embarrassment. So it doesn't really matter what I do, does it? The fact that I exist embarrasses him and there's no getting past that."

"I'm sure that's not true—"

"It is true," Mattea fired back at her, looking flushed with temper again. "Personally, I'm more than happy to live down to every single low expectation he has of me. I'm certainly not going to flail around, desperate for his approval like my mother. And if that means that you get fired too? I'll consider that a happy bonus."

"I will make a note," Beatrice said, watching the girl.

But Mattea was still going. "My brother is no different from my father or any other man. They think that every time they're ready to move on, they can erase the past, except I have a nasty habit of turning up." She let out a harsh laugh. "Like a rash."

Beatrice knew at once that someone had said that to her. Those exact words. And even as she understood that, she knew immediately that it hadn't been Cesare—because if it had been, she wouldn't have said it that way.

"If I'm going to be a rash, I'm going to be the itchiest, most unbearable rash there ever was," Mattea said in a hard sort of voice that sounded a lot as if she was trying to cover over the glint of emotion in her eyes. "This has been a nice try to attempt to win me over, Miss Higginbotham. But it's not going to work. You might as well give up now."

"Mattea," Beatrice replied, setting her tea down with a click, "you could not possibly say anything that would make me less likely to give up. Ever."

Mattea laughed again, in that harsh way. "That's what they all say," she bit out. "And yet they all do. One after the next, like clockwork. You'll be the same."

And despite everything—not least the child she was carrying inside her—Beatrice vowed there and then that she would not.

Because she could not help feeling for the girl, abandoned like this. So vulnerable and trying so hard to hide it.

She could not help but think about what she'd want for her own child if, God forbid, she wasn't here to care for the baby herself.

Thinking of her own child like Mattea, foisted off on someone who did not dote on her as surely as her mother had and would…

But Beatrice could not allow herself to entertain the emotions that swamped her then. She had to focus instead, and so she did.

On the one thing she could do here, and she vowed that she would. That she would help Mattea whether the girl wanted to be helped or not. That one way or another, she would not abandon this girl. No matter what.

Even if she had to fight Mattea's own brother to do it.

CHAPTER FOUR

SINCE HE HAD installed the confounding headmistress in his household, Cesare had not been aware of his sister in a negative sense at all. No tedious scenes over dinner, a danger to herself and the table settings. No attempts to disrupt his business calls at all hours. No reports of her behavior, delivered in sorrowful tones by Mrs. Morse when he returned from his many trips.

This suggested to him that he had done the right thing, as ever.

And so he had the woman brought before him for a status report at the end of the first week since he had assumed guardianship of Mattea, and she was in residence, that had been...quiet. Usually when his sister was in Tuscany, she made sure to paint the whole of the estate with her particular brand of chaos.

The headmistress herself, oddly haunting though she had appeared to him when they'd met, was doing her job. Nothing else mattered.

It was a lovely summer's night, warm and ripe with the scent of flowers on the breeze. Cesare had spent the afternoon locked away in his offices, wrapped up in a particularly tense set of negotiations with a business concern in the Philippines. He quite liked the heightened tension of high-level discussions but he liked this, too. Sitting out on his favorite terrace, the one with the sweeping views all the way down to the lake and beyond, enjoying *la bella vita* with an *aperitivo*, as the good lord surely intended a Chiavari to do.

Beside him on the small, tiled table, the staff had placed a selection of freshly baked *schiacciata*, tart olives and sun-dried tomatoes from his own land, and his favorite *pecorino*, though he was indulging only sparingly tonight. Later, he would fly up to the Côte d'Azur, where he had agreed to attend a weekend-long party in the house of an old friend and business associate. Cesare had never been much for parties, but this one was different. He was going to the party because Marielle was attending, and she expected him to propose.

He had indicated he might. It was high time he did.

And so he took these sweet, calm moments to sit here, looking out at the legacy in question, and let himself think of how nice it would be to take the next step. To settle the enduring question of who he would marry, and when, and apply himself to the next phase.

Cesare knew it was time because it no longer felt like an imposition. It felt like a piece to a long-unsolved puzzle, snapping into place at last. For it would mean that he had followed his late father's instructions to the letter.

The literal letter.

He no longer carried it with him everywhere he went, but the letter his father had written him so that he might have it long after the old man's death stayed in pride of place in Cesare's office. He kept it tucked just beneath the glass of his workspace, so that he could always be reminded of his father's advice and allow it to be his true north, always.

Vittorio had been elderly when Cesare was born, and Cesare had been off at boarding school for most of his youth. Vittorio had died while Cesare was sixteen and still studying abroad, but he had made certain that his son and heir knew his thoughts on how to maintain the Chiavari fortune, how to expand where possible and hold back when wise. He had advocated in the letter that Cesare wait until he was older and settled to bother with a wife.

Because, he wrote, *the risks are too great that a young man will think too little and act too rashly. An older man, having had all the experiences he might wish, will choose a mate that will benefit the family name above all things.*

What he had not written about was why he had chosen Cesare's mother, when he had only lost himself in jealous rages over her. Cesare had come to think of the letter as not only Vittorio's advice to his son, but a mea culpa over some of his less-than-stellar choices.

Cesare heard the sound of a door opening behind him and turned slightly so he could watch the approach of the headmistress closely. Almost with interest—except there was nothing to catch his interest. The woman was dressed, again, as if she was attempting to disappear in plain sight right there on the loveliest terrace in all of Italy.

Once he thought that, he found himself studying the oversize glasses that covered so much real estate on her face, wondering why anyone would need such a monstrous pair. Because it certainly wasn't for fashion, of that he was certain. There was nothing *fashionable* about her. She was a study in a certain brand of put-together drabness that offended him to the depths of his Italian soul.

He might have learned how to control himself and everything around him when he was still technically a teenager, but Cesare had grown up here. Right here, surrounded by what he confidently believed was the most beautiful bit of earth on the planet. He sought out beauty in whatever he did, wherever he went.

What he did not understand was a person who could have improved their appearance, yet did not.

As she came to stand before him, as round and owlish as he had convinced himself he had misremembered, he reminded himself that how she presented herself was no concern of his. The woman he'd hired to wrestle his problematic sister into good behavior whether Mattea liked it or not needed only to accomplish that. She could otherwise be as drab as she liked, with his blessing.

He beckoned for her to take the seat opposite him, there on the other side of the small table. She sank down in the chair with a surprising show of grace, and the strangest reaction rippled through him, making him frown. It wasn't only that a certain heat bloomed in him, confounding him, when she had displayed so little elegance. When she was so round he could not even manage to discern a figure beneath her garments at all.

That was concerning enough, as a man who considered himself something of a connoisseur when it came to stunning women, but there was something else. It was almost as if she reminded him of something, or someone—

But who could she possibly remind him of? He had only seen her on the day she'd arrived, and now. Perhaps he was simply remembering the way she'd come down the grand stairs, as if there was an elegance deep in her bones no matter what her station in life or what she chose to wear.

Of far more concern was that bizarre surge of attraction—but that he could chalk up to the unusual celibacy he had been practicing for months now.

In any case, he dismissed it.

"I have neither seen nor heard from my sister since your arrival," he said, waving a hand at the *aperitivo* that waited beside her to indicate it was hers. "I must congratulate you."

The headmistress frowned faintly at the drink, as if she thought it might lead her straight into a den of iniquity if she so much as touched the glass.

"I believe your sister is humoring me," she told him. And when she raised her gaze to his, she smiled. In that way of hers that was neither soothing nor placating, and as such, made him...something close enough to *uncertain* as to how he should respond.

He was Cesare Chiavari. He was never uncertain, by definition.

It was clear to him that her smile was a weapon.

"Humoring you?"

She sat back in her chair without surrendering the ruthlessly straight line of her spine, a feat he found himself admiring as if it was architectural. "I believe she is attempting to lull me into a false sense of security, so that her next act of defiance will seem all the more dramatic in comparison and, with any luck, also get me fired."

He considered that. And this strange woman who, everything in him stated with no hesitation, he should not be sitting around with like this. For any reason.

She is dangerous, something in him whispered, but it was connected to that inconvenient heat. He had no choice but to do his best to shove it aside. Hard.

"Do you know what this act of defiance will entail?"

"We have to assume that her target is always you, Mr. Chiavari." She folded her hands in her lap, managing to look serene and something like regal, for an owl. If not remotely comfortable. "It's understandable that you are the focal point for these displays." He must have looked confused, or perhaps irritated, because her brows rose. "Surely the care and interest you have given so generously while raising her marks you as her only remaining family member in any real sense."

And it had been a very long time since anyone had dared attempt to chastise him. So long, in fact, that he could not remember it ever occurring. Cesare was astonished to find that he felt the faintest hint of something like *chagrin* trickle through him.

"Are you suggesting that I do not care for my own sister?" He did not say *Do you dare?* His tone said it for him.

She did not appear to notice. "I believe I said the exact opposite."

"But it was the way you said it, Miss Higginbotham."

Again, that sharp smile. "You must have misunderstood me." He had not. "I am well used to girls like your sister. They all come to the school in the same state. What we try to do is redirect their energies toward more appropriate outlets."

"And what might that be?" He laughed. "Do you imagine she will take up watercolors? The piano? Perhaps we ought to encourage her to *journal*, is that it?"

The woman eyed him, again in a way that made

him feel slightly discomfited. "Do you think those are the only acceptable outlets for feminine energy? You are aware, I hope, that this is not the Victorian age?"

"Tell me something." And though he never spoke without knowing exactly where the conversation should go, tonight, somehow, he felt less careful. That, too, felt uncomfortably familiar. "Why are you no longer with the school? I found the statement issued in the wake of your departure notably uninformative."

"I wanted a change," she said, after a moment in which he wondered if she planned to answer him at all. "And no, before you ask, I had no desire to take *this* job. I was thinking more along the lines of something charming that could be left behind at the end of the day. I have long wondered what sort of life *that* must be."

"Boring," Cesare said softly. He didn't mean to.

Her gaze flew to his, and for a moment, something snapped into place between them, and it was more than a memory. It was like a switch being pulled—

But she aimed that bland smile at him again. "You made me an offer I felt I could not refuse."

He felt that switch snap back into place and could not have said why he resented it when he didn't even know what it was for. "It is cheering to know that your morals are no better than anyone else's, I suppose. You are as avaricious as the rest."

"Yes," she said, with that smile at the ready and

sharper than before, to his mind. "Of the two of us sitting here, I am the one awash in avarice. You can tell, because you are the lord and master of all you survey. And I sleep in your attic in a room I doubt you have ever entered. But truly, you and I are the very same."

That might have been a stinging critique—he felt sure it was meant to be, and there were parts that landed on him hard, but that had more to do with imagining her asleep—but then she laughed. And he was not prepared for the sound.

It almost reminded him of another laugh he had heard once, musical and light, a stunning descant to a busker's cello on a bridge in Venice—

But this was far more pointed. More edgy, and Cesare had no idea why he was allowing that particular memory to pollute his head once more. It had been one night. He was not in the habit of one-night stands, because he was a creature of habit. He preferred regular sex to adventures with uncertain outcomes. He had told himself that it was far better to lock that night away, and he had succeeded.

It had been months now.

Yet another truth was that he'd woken up to find her gone, that mystery woman in Venice, and he had looked for her with a ferocity that he had never displayed for anything else. Or anyone else.

He did not particularly care for that truth.

He had never been a man of passion, not before that night. Not since.

And in any case, it was all for the best that he'd never been able to find the woman he'd met by chance that night. The woman who had melted all over him like fire and silk, and whose innocence had been as miraculous as it was unexpected. A woman who, he had come to think, must have been in a similar situation to his. With a set future before her, like it or not, and only the one, stolen night to pretend otherwise.

He did not like to think about that, either.

But what Cesare knew full well was that he was in no position to marry a woman who could tie him up in so many knots the way his companion had that night. He knew that passion was fleeting and that his true legacy was in the details he managed over the sweep of time. These were the lessons he had learned, not from his father's letter, but from an analysis of his father's life. His mother's life. His sister's father too.

Whole lives were ruined by the uncertainty of desire. His was not a life of uncertainty—that was its blessing and its curse. Some men in his position took up extreme sports. Fast cars, high mountains. Cesare had never developed the taste for such distractions, too cognizant had he always been that if he died, his family legacy died with him.

And he needed to protect that legacy and provide for it. He had no place in his life for a night like that, so filled with longing and need and something like magic that he could have been anyone. Not Cesare Chiavari at all.

Just a man like any other, struck down by a woman with a single, smoky-eyed glance.

It was all for the best that he had not been able to locate her. He knew that. He did.

"Whatever you are doing," he said in repressive tones as her laughter died away, as he tried to get rid of that unsettled feeling within himself, "I can only hope it continues."

"It won't." She lifted a hand and demonstrated, making it bob up and down like a dolphin. "There will be peaks and valleys. You cannot expect perfection."

He did not *glare*. He was not given to *glaring* at his staff. Still, he supposed the way he regarded her was stern. "I think you will find that I can. I do. I always expect perfection, Miss Higginbotham. That is what I am paying you to obtain here."

She did not look as abashed by that as he felt she should. She did not look abashed at all. "I understand that, but we are speaking of a fifteen-year-old girl with *feelings*. I can be as perfect as it is possible to be. She will not do the same. On that you can depend." Her lips curved as if she was holding back that laughter again. "Mr. Chiavari."

He found himself studying the woman as if she was a game of chess, and one he wished to win, when he could not recall ever feeling such a thing about a person in his employ before.

"What do you suggest should be done with her, then?" he asked.

Again, a curve of her lips, but he could still hear that damned laughter, as if it was *inside* him now. He was struck once more by how haunting it was when it should not have been. When she should have been anything but.

The woman looked like an owl, for God's sake.

"I don't know much about family relations, I'm afraid," she told him, with a disarming directness that he wanted to enjoy—but he knew by now that this woman only attempted a disarm when there were other weapons at her disposal. "I'm an orphan. Both of my parents were only children. So you see, I have never experienced the joys and challenges of the familial state."

"And yet you have worked with children all this time."

She tipped her head slightly to one side, as if he was the one who made no sense. "I don't think one is required to have a family to work with young people. In fact, most families who send their children to Averell do so because they cannot find a way to deal with the child in question. So perhaps it is the opposite. Perhaps I am better suited for the job."

"A job you gave up."

She took a moment to look out toward the hills. Then she turned that same assessing look on him. "I don't imagine you will be able to understand. Because of who you are, I imagine you must always be…this. Who you are. I imagine the person you would be was decided from birth."

"It is called duty," he told her. "And an abiding interest in my family's legacy, which stretches back into antiquity."

"I can see how that could be both a burden and a deep joy," she said, and he did not understand why that felt to him like a breath, finally released. "I have a duty only to myself and no legacy to speak of, save what I fashion as I go."

"That sounds very…untethered," he found himself saying.

Something in her gaze seemed to kindle then, suggesting sparks when there could be none, surely. No switches, no sparks. "But a tether is such an interesting thing, is it not? It can either be a binding, holding us against our will. Or it can be its own safety net, I suppose, holding us fast when we fear we might fall."

And Cesare wondered if it was the owlishness about her that made him wonder what the difference was between falling and flying free…and then cursed himself for his foolishness. He was not in a position to imagine anything of the kind. He had spent years settling on the appropriate wife and now that he'd located her, he needed nothing to stand in his way.

Especially not himself and this…nonsense.

"I will never know," he said, his tone harsh.

He didn't understand why it felt so easy, so natural, to talk with her like this. Of such odd and unnecessary things. Cesare did not normally sit about in the evenings, *conversing* with his staff. He gave directives and orders, and he was not available for explanations about failures when it came to carrying out those orders and directives. He took pride in the fact that he was not an unkind master, but he was always the master.

He could not think of a single time he had ever forgotten himself.

And he assured himself he was not forgetting himself now.

"I think it is easier for people like me to decide on a change," she said, as if she knew all the things he was thinking, when of course she couldn't. She couldn't begin to understand what it was like to be steeped in his own history with every breath, and to *like* that. To see it not as a terrible yoke, but as an opportunity. She was tetherless, as she had told him. An insubstantial creature with a life that would never be recorded into stone, as his would be one day, in the gallery of statues and in the family crypt. "I don't know how you would ever manage to be anything but who you are. The Chiavari heir and all that entails."

But unlike every other person who had said something like that to him, the round little owl beside him did not sound remotely admiring.

"I have no interest in change of any kind," he said, but there was something, then, in the way she gazed back at him. That hint of something sparking in her gaze, perhaps.

A kind of knowledge there that should not have existed.

And certainly should not have felt as if it was mirrored in him.

"Yet you are to be married," she said quietly.

And there was nothing off about the way she said it. What was off was his reaction. Something in him almost…prickled into attention.

But he was Cesare Chiavari and he did not *shiver* before a woman. Much less his own staff.

"I do not foresee my marriage being any kind of meaningful change," he told her, gruffly, after a moment. "Why should it be? It is merely a necessary continuation of the existing legacy of this family, this land. The empire that was built here."

A sort of amusement lit her gaze then. "What a lucky bride she will be, then, whoever she is. To disappear so completely into your…legacy."

He did not miss the emphasis she put on that last word, and could only hope he did not sound or look as affronted as he felt. "There are many women who would consider that a great honor."

"I have no doubt that there are." She paused, and for the faintest moment she looked almost uncertain. But then he thought he'd imagined it when she leaned slightly toward him, her expression intense and her huge glasses catching the evening light. "You do know that it does not have to be all one way or the other, don't you? You can create your own legacy without tearing down your family's. They're not in competition."

"Forgive me," he said through his teeth, "but you have no idea what you are talking about. How could you?"

There was something in the air between them then, making the lengthening shadows feel richer all around. Something in him felt electric, but he knew that must be a misinterpretation, because this was not the sort of woman who inspired such reactions in him. This was not the sort of woman to whom he should find himself telling secrets that he would otherwise assume were his to keep to the grave.

A sunset out on the most glorious terrace in Tuscany could not change that.

He would not let it, no matter what she seemed to know about him. She didn't *truly* know anything. He knew that. He knew she was only guessing.

Because that was all that this could be.

In any case, being unexpectedly seen and understood in that way—that had only happened the once.

It was all for the best, Cesare kept reminding himself, that he would never see his lady of Venice again. Because that stood as the only night in his life that he could recall actually imagining a different path forward. A different legacy altogether. He had held her sweet body close to his and he had slept, dreaming about all the ways he would change heaven and earth if he had to, if he could keep her.

He had no desire to relive those hours. They had rendered him unknowable to himself, and he could not abide it.

And it had been the height of foolishness, because the woman had disappeared without so much as telling him her name.

Cesare could not understand why this odd, inappropriate *owl* made him think about that night the way she did. He doubted she knew the first thing about passion and he wished he did not either. It was far too...messy.

He stood, abruptly, and that too was a betrayal of who he was. He had been trained in perfect manners since the time he was small. There was no reason at all he should abandon the habits of a lifetime simply because a headmistress he employed to handle his sister made him uncomfortable.

But he did not sit. Nor excuse himself.

"I have a plane to catch," he said.

And when her smile widened, it was as if he could hear the words inside her head, pointing out that one did not have to catch a plane that already belonged to him. That it was likely to wait as long as he wished it to.

Only once, in Venice, had a woman looked straight through him, but that night, he had enjoyed it. It had made him feel as if something molten flowed in his veins, and he had wanted nothing more than to burn with her.

Again and again.

Tonight he could not abide it. So he merely turned on his heel and stalked off of his own terrace. Cesare told himself that he was simply removing himself from an interaction that had gone on too long.

He was not running. He was not quitting his own house.

And by the time he made it out to the airfield, he had convinced himself that his reaction had been entirely proper. The headmistress was a maddening woman dressed like an owl and he was the master of the house. He did not have to descend to her level. It had been a compliment that he had condescended to do so for even a few moments, but he would not do so again.

Just as you will not think of that woman in red again either, an arch voice inside him whispered, sounding entirely too *headmistressy* for his taste.

It was a short flight to the Côte d'Azur, and another short drive into the hills above Nice for this party he had said he would attend. He was a man of his word, was he not? This was the only reason he could think of as to why he did not stop off at one of the medieval villages along the way.

This was the only reason he chose to ignore the notion that walking into this party was like fashioning his own noose.

But when he arrived, everything was as it should be, and there was no noose in sight. His friend's home was a sparkling château nestled in the more dramatic hills of Provence. It was a study in elegance, no de-tail too small or insignificant. His friend, who he had known since they were young boys in far-off England, was as amusing as Cesare recalled him. The friends and acquaintances he had gathered were the same. And Marielle, the heiress he had picked out to become his bride, shined like a well-set jewel in the middle of the expected splendor.

Everything was perfect. The food, the wine. The conversation was sophisticated, entertaining, and intelligent, and afterward, when there was dancing, Marielle moved in his arms like a song.

So there was no reason that later, when he found himself alone in the rooms that had been prepared for him, he found himself studying the ring he had brought with him for the occasion—unable to explain to his own satisfaction why he had not proposed.

It had been the perfect night for it. He had planned to ask her in the accepted way, not in the center of a dance floor but on a walk in the gardens, perhaps. And yet here he was, alone in his room and still without the fiancée he already knew would accept him.

Was desperate to accept him, by all accounts.

He threw open the French doors that led to the balcony off his bedchamber, wearing nothing but the boxer briefs he slept in when he was away from home, should he have to leap up and handle a fire, overly familiar fellow guests, or other such middle-of-the-night calamities.

It was cool, this high in the hills, and he liked the breeze on his skin. The moon was high in the sky, like a blessing, when what he felt like doing instead of praying was letting out a howl as if he was a wolf after all.

And maybe that strange image was what stuck with him when he finally took himself to bed, promising himself that he would address this strange issue he had created come morning. He would find Marielle and propose to her in sunlight, as if he had not disappointed her tonight.

That was what he told himself as he drifted off to sleep, but the moon shined in and got tangled up inside him, making him more wolfish than a dutiful man should permit himself to become. Maybe that was the reason why he did not toss and turn, but fell instead into a deep, rich dream.

It started off in Venice, as so many of his dreams did. But this time, when he brought his mystery woman back to his hotel, he knelt between her legs and drank deep of those sweet, hot mysteries at her core.

And he licked his way into her until she cried out, and he shocked himself awake.

Because when he looked up to see the face of his lover in that dream, he saw Headmistress Higginbotham instead.

CHAPTER FIVE

"SOMETHING IS DIFFERENT with my brother," Mattea said one morning, shuffling along beside Beatrice on what the surly teenager liked to call her daily forced march. Sometimes she even called it boot camp.

No matter what she called it, Beatrice only smiled, and walked faster.

"Perhaps he has gone ahead and become engaged," Beatrice suggested today, and if those words tasted sour on her tongue, she would never admit it. She would swallow them down, every bitter drop, before she gave the slightest indication that she cared what Cesare Chiavari did with himself, his life, or his betrothal.

This was why she insisted on morning walks out in nature. It was healing.

She was *healing*.

"Impossible," Mattea was saying with all of that overweening confidence of hers that she could produce at will. "He might like to keep it secret, obviously, because he's always ranting about escaping the glare of public interest, blah blah blah, but there's no way *she* would go along with that."

As if she knew the woman in question, was all Beatrice could think, when she'd been under the impression that Cesare was still in the process of choosing—

But none of this was her business. None of this concerned her at all.

When Beatrice did not reply, the younger girl sighed. "It's a fact that every woman in Europe has chased after my brother at one point or another. Whoever lands him will be celebrated far and wide. It will be called a coup. You must know this."

"I can't think of any topic that concerns me less than your brother's betrothal," Beatrice said icily, as much to remind herself as to get Mattea to drop the subject.

It had been almost a month now, here in this beautiful place that only seemed to root itself more deeply inside her by the day. But she had other things to worry about when it came to things *inside her*, thank you. Everyone loved Tuscany, but Beatrice's waist grew thicker and her belly protruded unapologetically, and at night she rubbed herself with lotions and was deeply grateful that she'd had the foresight to buy such baggy, oversize clothes that made her look twice her size anyway.

She only looked rounder now.

If asked, she would claim it was the endless supply of homemade pasta that accompanied every meal.

Beatrice expected she would dream about the handcrafted pasta here for the rest of her life.

What she would try to forget was that every week, Cesare called her before him and interrogated her about his sister's progress, whatever that was supposed to be. He was never as open as he'd been that first time, and she told herself she was grateful.

But she also didn't know what progress he was looking for from a teenager who was doing surprisingly well with the constant company of her former headmistress.

After all, she had said last time, with perhaps more asperity than necessary—in his office, because he'd never had her back to that glorious terrace at sunset, and thank goodness—*there are no exams to sit, are there? She will either disrupt your wedding or she won't.*

But now all she could think was that he had not corrected her. He had not said that he *wasn't* getting married, so she had to assume he still was. Even if privately she agreed with Mattea. If a man like Cesare had gotten engaged, the world would know.

I would know, something in her insisted, as if knowing the man she'd exulted in for only one night allowed her to know this cold man who'd taken his place, too.

"Maybe he won't get married after all." Mattea was speculating now as they took their usual route, out into the vineyards, out a little farther every day, and then back when Mattea started to get a bit fractious. Or remember that she *should*. "He doesn't really *need* to."

And it made Beatrice's heart hurt to hear the way the girl said things like that. With so much *hope* in her voice that it would have horrified her, if she could hear herself. It made Beatrice want to turn on her heel and charge back into the house so she could upbraid the man in question about the way he treated this little sister of his. This child who only wanted a relationship with him, no matter how she went about it.

But that was not her place.

And besides, there really was a change in Cesare, but Beatrice didn't think it had anything to do with his plans to marry. For all she would know or be told, the wedding could be next week. It had taken her a week or so to figure out what, precisely, it was that she was sensing during her meetings with him. And when he dropped into the little adventures she and Mattea took around the house and the grounds.

It is almost as if you are showing her how to treat this place, he said on one such occasion, coming up behind Beatrice and nearly making her jump. He had been looking past her toward his sister, who had been laughing with Amelia as the maid tried to teach her how to set a table in the formal style. *Did I hear that yesterday my sister learned how to do laundry?*

Beatrice had dared Mattea to try, claiming she would ruin all the garments and likely flood the house, but she didn't tell Cesare this.

Don't let your sister know it's educational, she whispered in mock horror. *That would ruin everything!*

She'd turned to look at him then and had found Cesare gazing at her in that way he'd been doing for weeks now. And she'd finally realized that it felt a lot like suspicion.

As if he was *actively suspicious* of her.

It told her things she was not sure she wanted to know about herself that her reaction to the possibility that he was onto her true identity—or anyway, the identity she'd flirted with in Venice, because she couldn't say that was her at all—filled her with more delight than despair.

You have been shockingly wrong about the content of your character your whole life, she told herself sternly. *It's only this past year that you have actually met your true self.*

And her true self, it turned out, was a bit shocking.

But these were not conversations she could have with Mattea, who she found she liked a great deal now that the girl was not playing to her classmates. But they were not friends. They could not be *friends*.

"Many men in your brother's position feel that they must marry," she told the girl now instead. And it was possible she was explaining that to herself, too. And the baby inside her. "They feel a tremendous duty to carry on the family line. I think you'll find this is the story of the world as we know it."

"It's stupid," Mattea replied, with an epic eye roll.

That Beatrice agreed with her was, of course, also not something she could share. She gave her charge a reproving look. "In the meantime, dare I hope that this spate of good behavior from you will continue? Last time I met with your brother, he asked if you were ill."

Mattea laughed, but there was color in her cheeks to Beatrice's eyes, and not from temper today. It was fresh air, maybe. Or far healthier emotions than usual.

"I'm too bored to bother," Mattea said, but she was biting back a smile at that lie. "Don't you worry, though. There's loads of time for me to meet every low bar Cesare has in place for me."

Beatrice thought about that later, during the evening quiet hours she'd instituted over the past weeks. Mattea had protested at first, bitterly, claiming she might wish to do things normal teenage girls did on a summer evening and sometimes that included music as well as a reasonable curfew. Beatrice had been unmoved.

You do not have a single friend in a hundred-mile radius, she'd said crisply. It was her feeling that Mattea had precious few friends at all, because she gravitated toward troublemakers like herself, who were always about the drama they could cause above all else. But she knew better than to share that observation. *So the only thing you could possibly do of an evening is get yourself into trouble. We will not be doing that.*

Maybe I want to watch a movie that it would be embarrassing to watch with my jumped-up governess. Maybe I want to hang about in chats or on video calls making up stories to tell my friends. Maybe I just want to be alone, she'd hurled back.

You can be alone all you like, as long as I know where you are, Beatrice told her serenely. *You can listen to whatever music you choose, using headphones. If you want to interact, I will teach you how to play games that, yes, you can weaponize in various ways when you're older. I suggest you worry about your own reaction to any movies, not mine. If you wish to send sulky and insulting texts to your friends, presumably about me, by all means. Feel free to do so, but you will do it while sitting in the same room as me. These are the rules.*

Mattea had won herself extra quiet hours that day for her profane response to that.

But she had settled into the routine Beatrice imposed upon her with surprising ease. Sometimes they did actually play games. Sometimes they watched movies in her media room, though they got less provocative once the girl realized Beatrice refused to give her the reactions she wanted. And many nights featured Mattea performatively typing into her mobile or her laptop for many hours while Beatrice caught up on her reading.

Lately Beatrice had begun to think that there was probably more to this run of good behavior on Mattea's part than the rules Beatrice had set down.

It wasn't that Mattea was suddenly filled with the desire to be obedient.

It was that she was the most outrageous when she had an audience, for one thing. And for another, it was that this might very well be the only time she'd ever had somebody else's full attention.

"Did you spend a great deal of time with your mother while she was alive?" Beatrice asked one afternoon while dealing a hand of cards.

Mattea swiped up her cards and fanned them out before her. "When she was around, I guess."

"Did you do mother-daughter things? Did you have traditions?"

"I told you she liked to have her little *afternoon soirees*. She would dress me up and teach me how to be delightful." Mattea made a face, frowning at Beatrice over the top of her cards. "Why are you asking me this?"

Beatrice gazed back at the girl, trying to keep her expression impassive as her heartbeat picked up speed. Why *was* she asking such things? She told herself it was because she cared about Mattea, but even as she did, she knew there was more to it.

Maybe she simply wanted to hear what it was like to have a mother for longer than she'd had hers. Maybe she wanted to soak in that bond, no matter what it was like, so she could figure out how to love her own baby as well as possible.

She cleared her throat. "My mother died when I was seven. I remember when I was very small, she'd read me stories. When I was a little older, we would go on walks in the evening and we would talk about the days we had. It made me feel very grown-up."

Mattea didn't actually sneer, but it was a close call. "That sounds sweet, really," she said, making it clear she thought it was anything but. "That's not the kind of mother mine was."

"How was she, then?"

"My mother threw parties or she went to parties. So she slept all day, woke up in the afternoon, spent hours getting dressed, and then went out. She made me sit with her while she was getting dressed, so she could teach me how to be a sultry and alluring woman. She would spray me in perfume and make me taste her champagne. She taught me how to dance for a lover when I was eight. Sometimes she liked to take pictures of the two of us, but only when she looked young and fresh. But none of this made me feel like I was a grown-up." Her blue eyes were hard and sad when they found Beatrice's. "More like I was her pet hamster."

It cost her a lot not to react to any of that the way she wanted to, because showing the girl the deep compassion she felt—and the anger she wished she could share with a dead woman who should have treated her daughter better—would only make Mattea recoil. She knew that appearing nonchalant was the only way to keep her talking. "And what about your father?"

"Oh, he forgot he had a kid." Mattea shrugged

when Beatrice only gazed back at her. "He always seemed surprised to see me. Too surprised. You know."

Beatrice had to bite her tongue as she discarded some cards and picked up others.

"It was always the most fun when Cesare visited," the girl said a few moments later, unprompted. "I thought it would be like that all the time when I came to live with him, but it's not."

"And why do you think that is?" Beatrice asked her.

Mattea looked at her, then looked down. "I know what I'm like, Miss Higginbotham. And so do you."

Then she was done with cards in a sudden, swift storm of a mood change. She threw hers onto the table and whirled around, making her way back to her favorite couch and curling up with her mobile, refusing to look up again until late.

You can't make me go to bed just because you tell me to, Mattea had shouted at her on one of the first nights. *I'm fifteen. I'm not a child.*

You can sneak out if you want to, Beatrice had replied, unfazed. *But I have instructed the staff to deliver you to me when they catch you out and about. If I can't trust you to stay in your room, Mattea, I will make you sleep on the floor in mine. How does that sound?*

My brother will never allow it, the girl had snapped.

But she also hadn't snuck out since, apparently not wishing to test the theory.

Now that they had discussed emotions and family dynamics and had almost managed to get into Mattea's self-worth, Beatrice supposed everything was back on the table. And so, when she made her typical nightly announcement that it was bedtime and that she would be leaving Mattea to make good choices, she didn't go up to her rooms.

She went downstairs instead, smiling when she encountered Mrs. Morse in the servants' stair.

"Off to bed?" the older woman asked, because she knew everyone's schedule down to the minute.

"I have a feeling that tonight might be a night that Mattea attempts something," Beatrice said. "I thought I'd position myself in the best possible place to apprehend her."

Mrs. Morse sighed. "She has been worryingly quiet of late," she agreed. "Follow me. I'll show you where she normally climbs down."

It was another beautiful summer evening outside. The stars were out, crowding the sky. Beatrice went and found herself a bench to sit on in the gardens, tucked back in the shadows but with a full view of Mattea's bedroom windows one story up.

But while she waited for the teenager's inevitable attempt to *do something*, what she thought about was Cesare.

And that particularly narrow, assessing way he'd been looking at her lately.

She blew out a breath, not surprised to feel it thick and tight in her throat.

He wasn't engaged yet. Not yet.

She knew he wasn't.

It was her secret shame that she looked every morning on her mobile before she got out of bed. Every morning before she rose, washed, and loved on her baby belly in the only place she could. In private. Before she stopped being a mother to the child she carried and became the headmistress. Before she twisted back her hair until her eyes watered, stuck on her glasses, and wore billowy clothes to hide herself.

And it was shameful enough that she looked.

But it was nothing short of sad that every day she woke without news of his betrothal, she felt hopeful.

The same way her fifteen-year-old charge had sounded hopeful that he might decide not to marry at all.

Maybe it was more than simply *shameful*. Maybe it was pathological.

"It is a lovely evening," came Cesare's voice, as if she'd imagined him out of the stars above and the faint breeze that danced over the garden, bringing with it hints of rosemary and night-blooming flowers.

She almost thought she was dreaming, but when she pinched herself, she was still there, sitting still on that bench in the garden. And Cesare was melting his way out from the shadows deeper in the garden, where the hedges were higher, and she heard there had once been a maze.

As if he'd been out on a night constitutional for,

perhaps, the same reason she marched around in the mornings.

Her heart took up a terrible knocking deep in her chest.

But she made herself smile at him primly, the way she always did. "It's beautiful, but then, it's always beautiful here."

She could hardly recall what she was agreeing to.

"I did not realize you enjoyed sitting out and taking the night air," he said, prowling closer.

There was no other word for how he was moving, though Beatrice tried desperately to find one. Because there was no need for her to be reacting to him as if he was some kind of big jungle cat, stalking her where she sat. That could lead nowhere good.

She refused to let herself think about dancing with him in Venice. In that packed little venue. On a bridge by themselves.

Then again, back in his room.

Where he had talked of passion and then taken her through an exploration of it.

Maybe the truth, obvious to her out here in the soft night that blurred everything, was that she hated that this was the same man. She *hated* it.

And she hated that he couldn't see her for who she was.

Yet none of these thoughts were the least bit productive.

Beatrice folded her hands in her lap and sat up straighter, trying to exude so much virtue that some of it sank into her, too. "I'm not sure I've ever met someone who did not enjoy a starry night, Mr. Chiavari."

He seemed to study her for moment too long, then another.

And then he confounded her completely by sitting down beside her.

Too close, she thought in a panic. He was too close, and she could not allow that. Because she knew how much closer they could get—

Seize hold of yourself, Beatrice ordered herself then. *All he sees is a servant.*

"I think it's time you call me Cesare," he suggested, another shock. "After all, Beatrice, you and I are involved in the same great enterprise, are we not?"

And she had not let herself wonder what it would be like to hear her name on his tongue. To yearn for it. She had not thought she ever would. It was like honey. It was like heat, and it was everywhere. It was far, far better and more seductive than she could possibly have anticipated.

It was a disaster.

"I'm perfectly happy to maintain formality between us," she told him, with less control than she would have liked.

"I think not," was all he said.

Beatrice made herself sit perfectly still. She could feel her internal temperature rocket up to something more akin to a forest fire, but there was nothing she could do about that. She gripped her laced fingers tightly, so tightly that it hurt, but she would never forgive herself if he knew these things that were happening to her. If he could *see*.

She did her best to exude a cool she didn't feel, and for the first time since she'd assumed the headmistress's position years ago, she wasn't sure it worked.

"You are, of course, the final word on all things," she said, agreeing with him in that way she knew was its own arch provocation.

She was not prepared for the rough caress of his laughter, dancing on the breeze. She hadn't heard that since Venice. Not in real life, anyway. Though she knew, the moment she heard it, that it was the song in her head, every morning when she opened her eyes.

It was a trap, she told herself.

But she didn't stand up and walk away, the way a wise woman would have.

"I'm delighted that you accept that I'm the person in charge," he said, after a moment. "As if there was some doubt."

Beatrice didn't understand what was happening, but as her head seemed to spin this way and that, she had to think that this had something to do with the way he'd been studying her lately. She didn't let herself imagine it had something to do with his delayed engagement, because that was madness.

But even though he disconcerted her simply by existing, she had become quite talented at hiding that. Or she hoped she had.

She concentrated on her posture. On the undeniable coolness of her tone. "I anticipate that at any moment, your sister will climb out of one of her bedroom windows," she told him matter-of-factly. "I made the very great mistake of prodding at her emotions and I imagine her reaction to that will be to get herself back into trouble as quickly as possible, because that feels much better. More familiar."

"I would think it would be the opposite. That getting into trouble would be the more emotional path."

"Getting into trouble allows a person to focus on who is to blame for doling out any consequences," Beatrice told him in the tone she reserved for junior staff. She was trying not to use her nose, because the scent of him was *just there*, like the breeze. Pine and rosemary and something warmer. Something she knew tasted deeper and richer when she had her mouth on him. It was entirely him. She felt her breasts grow heavy beneath her drapey clothes. "And to think deeply on how misunderstood one is, etcetera. Discussing emotional things is much harder. It requires a person to be vulnerable and most people avoid that at any cost."

"But not you, Beatrice. You have somehow transcended the reactions of mere mortals."

Her smile felt a bit brittle, but she aimed it at him anyway. "Not at all," she said. "The fact is that I have always recognized my vulnerabilities. Being orphaned will do that to you."

"You do realize that I am also an orphan, do you

not?" Again, that laugh of his that cascaded through her like sunlight. "Though I will admit, I do not consider myself one. Still, both of my parents are dead."

She actually turned and frowned at him then, though she knew that wasn't wise. "You are an extraordinarily wealthy orphan, and I think you know that. I, on the other hand, was an extremely poor one. With no options. I made my own way in this world. Added to that, I'm a woman. And women are always more aware of their vulnerabilities. That is the way of the world."

"You are not the only person alive who misses their parents, Beatrice."

That stung. Deeply. She sucked in a breath, and her hands clenched in her lap were more like a single fist. "I never said anything like that. I never *thought* anything like that."

But he had turned toward her, too, and this should not have been happening. "I will not claim that there are no privileges, but they come with a high price. Is that vulnerable enough for you? Or would you prefer that I tell you, step by step, what it was like to be eighteen years old and suddenly in charge of the vast Chiavari empire while I knew that all the while the world was holding its breath, waiting for me to fail?"

Beatrice would love him to do just that, but that was dangerous ground. And she was already afraid she would never be able to walk away from this garden bench in the moonlight. She was already afraid she'd come face-to-face with the real trouble here.

She didn't want to.

"And if you did fail, what would happen?" she asked him, fighting for her usual calm tones and not quite getting there. "You'd be slightly less rich, that's all. You and I are not the same." She blew out a breath. "But that doesn't make up for losing your parents. I'm sorry."

And she thought she heard his breath, like a sharp inhale.

"It shocks me, Beatrice, that you have spent all these years catering to the whims of these people you so despise." But now he was the one using a deeply sardonic tone. He moved closer and she could suddenly no longer see the stars above, so broad were his shoulders. So intensely did he regard her. And then, impossibly, his fingers were on her chin, tilting her face toward his. Just like that night months ago. "What do you think that precious school of yours would say if I were to tell them that all this time, you have been a wolf in hiding?"

And somehow, she was no longer sure that he was talking about the same thing she was. All she was conscious of was the danger. It seemed insurmountable.

And it, too, felt like that hot, sweet honey inside her.

She pulled back, and then stood. And told herself she could not afford to allow herself to process the touch of his fingers against the skin of her face.

Not now. Maybe not ever.

Not while she carried his baby deep inside her, and he looked at her as if he'd never laid eyes on her before.

Although, though she knew it must be a trick of the darkness, he did not appear to be looking at her like that just now. "I don't work there anymore," she reminded him, as gently as she could. "So you may tell them whatever you wish. And if our arrangement is no longer working for you, I would ask only that you pay me for time served and I'll be on my way."

She didn't mean that. She didn't think she did. It came out of her mouth without warning, but she kept herself from showing any surprise.

"I will decline that offer," he said, with hints of laughter in his voice.

He was going to be her undoing.

Again.

Everything in her pulled tight, because she was sure he was going to leap to his own feet and advance upon her once more, and Beatrice thought she would die if he did. She knew she would die if he didn't.

But instead, he laughed again, and that was worse.

Or better, something in her whispered.

But with a jut of his chin, he directed her attention to the house. To Mattea's windows.

That easily, he reminded her where they were. And what she ought to have been paying attention to. Because Mattea was climbing over the side of her balcony, dressed like some kind of fashion-conscious burglar. Complete with a beanie set *just so* on her blond head, though it was not cold by any measure.

Beatrice didn't mean to—surely she didn't *mean* to—but she drifted back toward the bench, back into the shadows, closer to Cesare.

"Where do you think she imagines she's going?" Cesare asked, his voice low.

"She's well aware that there's nowhere to go," Beatrice said quietly. She folded her arms in front of her, aware that her breasts were tender, and felt swollen, and she could pretend all she liked but she knew it wasn't her pregnancy. Not when she could feel that bright, blooming heat between her legs. "So I have to assume that she has some mischief in mind."

"And what do you, in your infinite wisdom as headmistress extraordinaire, imagine we should do about this?"

Beatrice had never felt less wise in her life. If anything, she felt a strange kinship with Mattea because, deep down, there was no getting away from the fact that she wanted this man's attention too. If she'd been *wise* she would've walked away from this place the moment she'd seen that he didn't know who she was.

But it was too late for all that, so instead she tried to think tactically, knowing what she did about Mattea specifically and teenage girls in general. "She wants your undivided attention and I'm guessing she only gets it when you're furious with her."

"Are you suggesting—again—that I neglect my own sister?"

She shot him a look, but didn't answer that question. "I think part of her good behavior of late has been because she had *my* undivided attention," she said instead. "If I think critically about the year she spent in Averell, I have to conclude that what she's looking for is the full, irrevocable, and undeniable attention of the authority figure in every situation she's in. I assume none of that was available with her parents."

He was silent beside her, and Beatrice cautioned herself. She didn't know him. She might have spent a night with him, but that didn't mean she knew anything about what might be happening in his head *now*.

Though she did.

Because he proved it the next breath. "However neglectful you might imagine I am," he said in a low voice that left a few marks in every place it touched her, "let me assure you, it bears no resemblance to the total lack of regard in which she was raised."

It was only then she realized that there was a trembling, deep inside her, and the fact she was keeping it locked deep inside her didn't make it any better.

"What I suggest is a little bit of a mind game." Beatrice didn't look at him. She didn't dare. She wasn't sure she could count on her own restraint tonight. "If I've read your sister right, she will start attempting acts of defiance and destruction. I suggest we quietly put out whatever fires she sets—hopefully only metaphorically—and never mention them at all."

"That is the very opposite of doing one's duty and learning the consequences of one's actions," he growled at her.

"It is not a tactic I would take with *you*," she retorted without thinking. "But I think it has a very real chance of getting inside your sister's head in a way a lecture never will. She's already heard every lecture there is."

His eyes were too blue, hinting at all that passion she knew was there. She'd felt it. She'd lost herself in it. And she was not strong enough for this. For this coldness where so much heat should have been. She had never been strong enough for this. For him.

But she made herself pretend she was anyway, the way she always did.

Beatrice smiled as if nothing Cesare did concerned her in the least. "Of course, the choice is yours."

CHAPTER SIX

BEATRICE READ HER charge's intentions absolutely right, Cesare was forced to admit. He told himself he was delighted that he had chosen the right headmistress for the job. He told himself he had believed in her all along—or he would not have authorized his man to pay her as much as he was paying her.

That night they'd met in the garden, Mattea had snuck out by climbing down the side of the house using the trellis and an evidently too-hardy vine. When she hit the ground, she wandered into one of the outbuildings and trashed it.

Cesare had the place quietly set to rights before morning and had instructed the staff to say nothing about it. And later that same day Beatrice informed him, with that smile of hers, that Mattea seemed almost spooked by that response. That *lack* of response that was far louder than any threats or lectures.

Which was precisely what they wanted, she claimed.

Not that it kept Mattea from trying again. And again.

But every time his sister acted out, no matter how

big or bad the behavior, Cesare did the same thing and had it handled before morning. He set guards on her windows to track her nighttime trail of destruction, though he warned them to never let her see them. And slowly, Mattea's attempts to wreak a little bit of havoc…ebbed.

Before his eyes, without a single thundering lecture or threat of such things as incarceration, he watched his sister's entire demeanor shift.

What he could not understand was why he was so annoyed.

Or rather, he understood that it was Beatrice herself who was getting to him, personally, for all the same reasons he could not explain. Not the success she was having with his impossible sister. He was thrilled about that. But the way she mystified *him* without even seeming to try.

Then again, not understanding Headmistress Beatrice Higginbotham, or her effect on him, was becoming a significant issue all around. As was that dream, which kept coming back to him no matter how he tried to exhaust himself to keep it at bay.

That night in the garden he'd thought he *was* dreaming when he'd seen her sitting there in the dark, like the very fantasy he'd been trying to walk out of his head.

The walking wasn't working.

But since then, he'd avoided more shadows with her, too.

"If I may raise a personal matter," the woman

herself said in that prim, arch way of hers at one of their weekly meetings. It was coming on to the end of July by then. And he could not help but notice that she had taken on an internal sort of shine. He found it deeply disturbing, which was to say, he could not look away. Cesare was fairly certain that if he set her next to the moon, she would have out-glowed it.

And then he was forced to question where such terrible poetry was coming from, deep in his historically unpoetic soul.

"That is highly irregular," he said in quelling tones. "But I will allow it."

Her hazel eyes met his across the width of his desk. And held. "This job was presented to me as a temporary one. Predicated entirely on your betrothal, and then your wedding. I was given to understand that this would all happen in the course of the summer. This summer."

Cesare could not have said why he disliked, so intensely, that a round little owl—who seemed to get ever rounder by the day, to his eye—should mention the betrothal that hadn't happened yet. Or the wedding he should have started planning already.

Just as he could not comprehend how he, who had never dragged his feet where his duty was concerned, had now been doing so for months.

He gazed at her with as much arrogant amazement as he could manage. "I'm struggling to understand how or why this is a topic of conversation you feel is appropriate to raise with me."

"It will be August tomorrow," she said, in that gently intense way she used on Mattea all the time. Cesare did not appreciate the comparison. "Time is running out."

He sat back in his chair, pleased—and that was the right word, he assured himself—that he had moved their meetings to his office. Better to keep things on the right foot with no more meetings on a lovely terrace at sunset. Better to make sure his father's letter was at hand. Even if they were having an inappropriate conversation about his personal life anyway. "Do you imagine that I will have any trouble marrying in whatever timeline, accelerated or otherwise, that I wish?"

Her eyes seemed to glitter. "I only want to make sure that you're aware that *my* timeline cannot go past August." When he raised a brow, he thought she nearly flushed, then wondered why he wanted her to. What that would *mean*. "That was the agreement that was made."

There was no reason that should scrape at him. What did he care what life this woman had waiting for her out there, wherever she was from?

"As it happens, I have decided to throw a great party," he found himself saying. "My intended will be here, of course. I thought perhaps I might use this party as an opportunity to propose." He stared at her. "If, that is, my plans for my personal life meet with *your* approval, Miss Higginbotham."

And he didn't think he was the only one who felt the tension in the room, then.

"I'm sorry if I overstepped," Beatrice replied, and she sounded appropriately apologetic. But there was that way she was looking at him. There was that challenging glint in her gaze. He doubted very much that she was apologetic at all. "My interest in the matter is only in how it relates to my calendar. You understand."

He did not understand.

Just as Mrs. Morse did not understand when he informed her, perhaps a bit shortly, that he intended to throw a gala.

"You mean next year, surely?" the woman sputtered.

When she never sputtered.

"I mean next week," Cesare growled.

He had hired the indomitable housekeeper when he was leaving England, and his schooling, so he could come back to Italy and somehow take charge of the Chiavari empire. She had been overseeing the domestic workings of an entire public school's worth of posh boys, all of them neck-deep in too many pedigrees to count. At eighteen, he had thought she was a marvel.

He still did.

She proved herself to be exactly that when all she did was force a smile. "Everyone adores a summer party, Mr. Chiavari."

And she set about making it happen.

Most people could not throw a grand party on a moment's notice and expect anyone of worth to attend. Certainly not in the depths of summer, when so many people were committed elsewhere and had been for months.

But he was Cesare Chiavari. People would always do his bidding. Besides, most of Europe would kill for the opportunity to have a nose about the famous Chiavari estate, known for generations as the jewel of Tuscany. To prove his magnanimity, and perhaps to predispose her to consider behaving, he even told Mattea that she could invite some friends.

And yet as the party drew closer, he was…not right.

If he was a different sort of man, he might have called it agitation. But Cesare did not get agitated. He did not allow himself that lack of self-control.

Still, he found himself awake late into the night, holding that ring in his hand and turning it this way and that as if a new view of it might change things.

But no matter how hard he tried, he could not imagine it on Marielle's slender fingers.

When he thought of the ring that had once belonged to the grandmother who had died before he was born, he thought instead of the hands he'd seen clenching down hard into the bedcovers in his Venetian hotel. The fingers that had scraped their way down his back, leaving marks that had taken a long time to heal.

Marks he had missed once they were gone.

And worse by far, every time he closed his eyes, every time he drifted off to sleep, he dreamed of Beatrice.

Something about the woman drove him absolutely mad.

None of it made sense.

But Cesare was certain he had mastered it the night of the party.

Because he needed it mastered. Tonight was the night he would propose to Marielle, making her the next Chiavari wife, and ushering in the next era of the family legacy.

He should have been filled with the deep contentment that came from taking one more step toward the future he'd always known awaited him, the way he had at the start of the year. Back when he'd decided that it was time to stride with confidence into the next phase. The phase that had always been planned for him.

Cesare told himself that was exactly what he felt. *Contentment.* Though tonight it seemed like nothing so much as a deep pressure in his chest.

The guests had been trickling in all day, taking up residence in the guest quarters here in the house and in cottages spread out all over the property. The staff had prepared the estate, making it sparkle even more than it usually did, and Mattea—perhaps in anticipation—had kept her nighttime activities to the barest minimum. The last night she'd snuck out she'd only gone and sat by the lake for a time. There had been no cleanup crew required.

Perhaps you should view it as a gift for your betrothal, that infernal headmistress had suggested.

Now Cesare stood at the bottom of the grand stairs, waiting for the night—and his future—to begin. *Content* straight through. And as he watched, Marielle started down one side of the Y-shaped stair, making her way down from the guest wing side of the gallery. She was dressed to shine, and she took her time with each step, no doubt expecting that he would take the opportunity to appreciate her.

He did, Cesare assured himself. Of course he did.

From the other side of the gallery, Mattea ran down the opposing arm of the Y, entirely too fast for anything approaching the propriety she ought to show, given her position. He frowned at her as she shot past him, but he didn't bother to react to the insolent face she made.

His gaze was caught by the woman who followed after her, dressed in what he assumed must be a formal version of her usual shroud, hair scraped back and what looked like the faintest hint of lip color somewhere beneath her monstrous glasses.

And suddenly, irrevocably, he was faced with an unpleasant truth he had been avoiding for a very long time.

To the left, there was Marielle. She was all that was elegant. The sort of woman men wished to possess simply because she looked like what she was:

expensive and exclusive and out of most men's reach. Blonde and slim and tall, she glided instead of walking. She had the sort of long neck that was made to showcase dramatic jewels. She had a pleasing face that would always look good in a photograph. She knew precisely how to style herself to look her best at every occasion. She made a good impression without even trying.

And to the right was a woman who looked like nothing so much as an owl, feathers ruffled in perpetual outrage—or, perhaps, condemnation. She was decidedly round. She dressed in dark-colored shrouds and would look like a dark orb in any picture. Her glasses had ridiculously heavy frames that hid most of her face. She was not precisely a servant, but she wasn't a guest, either, and even the usually unimpressed Mrs. Morse had indicated that she liked the headmistress. Like everyone else in the house who was not a surly teen.

Yet it was a truth he could no longer deny that he spent uncountable hours imagining what it would be like to get his hands into that strict bun of hers and let her hair fall free. He had spent many, many nights wondering what her hair even looked like. Was it long? Thick? Did it curl when left to its own devices?

And that was but one, small fraction of his obsession with the woman.

He didn't understand it, but it had been happening for a while. And only now, faced with both Marielle and Beatrice practically side by side, could he accept this thing that baffled him as much as it made him uncomfortably hard.

He did not want the woman he intended to marry. Not like this. Not with a deep hunger that seemed to have no bottom.

Cesare wanted that little owl.

In a manner he would call *desperate*, if he were someone else.

And sometimes, in moments like this one, when her steady gaze was on his and something in the hazel depths glittered, he suspected she knew it.

But it was not as if that knowledge was any help to him. Not now. *Not ever,* a voice in him growled.

For any number of very good reasons, but particularly the blonde, lovely, and blue-blooded reason who glided down the rest of the stairs to stand before him. Presenting herself for an inspection that she likely expected would end in adoration.

What was the matter with him that he could not give even that to her?

"I have very few requirements," Marielle said quietly after a moment. "But one of them is that you at least *try* to pay attention to me when we are alone."

And she said that with her winning smile, the one that he could tell was lovely but left him cold. Because it turned out that what he wanted in a smile was a bit of weaponry. A dangerous edge, a hint of chastisement or judgment. Not centuries of breeding, apparently, with the perfect manners to match.

As he thought these things, his little owl passed

behind them, and Cesare realized that she existed completely beneath his intended's notice.

The way she should have existed beneath his.

"My apologies, Marielle," he murmured, drawing her arm through his. "I will attempt to focus my attention where it ought to go."

But he didn't. Because Cesare was aware of the typically determined sound of Beatrice's footsteps as she disappeared, ducking out of the great hall into one of the open, airy salons that flowed one into the next, clearly in search of Mattea and the friends who'd joined her for the weekend.

If he was not so afflicted by his own round, drab owl, Cesare would pay no more attention to the doings of his sister. He would assume that the person he'd hired to handle her was doing the job.

And yet as he led Marielle into the salon where the most important guests were already gathering ahead of the banquet, none of them fifteen-year-olds, he found he could barely track the conversation. Instead, he wondered if this was what he had to look forward to for the rest of his life. All of this gentility and talking around things, or past them. It had never occurred to him that cocktail conversation was nothing more than a means of passing the time. And that the fact that there were those who felt that it should be elevated to an art—and judged those who could not manage the task—suggested that the people indulging in such pastimes were idle enough that they required a certain kind of wit to animate the time allotted to conversations like this, because they had little else to do with it.

He stood slightly back from the group, watching Marielle play games he knew she'd been coached in since the cradle. She was good at all of it, of course. It was one of the criteria he had judged her on.

She had gotten high marks across the board. She was innocent, but had not spent her formative years locked away in a tower, like some. She was bright, educated. She was a keen runner and enjoyed testing her times in the races she ran. She'd had multidisciplinary interests at university yet had gone into charity work upon graduation, though not the way so many other heiresses did. She was not merely marking time. The charity she worked with was more hands-on and she'd spent a significant amount of time getting her hands dirty. And while Cesare did not require a wife with dirty hands, he admired her dedication.

But most importantly, Marielle had been raised to prize a strong legacy above all things. She had her own. As many questions as he had asked her about her future prospects, she'd had the same number of queries for him. She'd wanted to know what it would mean to be a Chiavari, how her children would be received by the world, and how best they could craft a life for them that could honor both of their august bloodlines.

She was a woman who knew her worth and expected her treatment to match.

And yet as he watched her shine in her own inimitable way, all Cesare could think was that she was…a lovely chandelier, made to give off good light, but always dependent on her surroundings to reach full strength.

He broke away from the group and told himself it was only because he, as host, needed to greet the rest of the guests. But he made short shrift of that and soon found himself moving through the parade of salons until he found the little huddle of teenagers in the one farthest away from the one he'd been standing in.

And Beatrice was there in the middle, somehow managing to have all the magic and mystery of moonlight. As if she was the moon itself.

She saw him coming and walked away from the group, but not before muttering a few words that Cesare did not have to hear to know were sharp.

"Surely you have better things to do, Mr. Chiavari, than monitor the children," she said crisply. Likely to make sure the teenagers heard her refer to them as children.

Because *this* woman did not appear to concern herself with him or his wishes at all, and he should have hated that.

Cesare knew that under any other circumstances, with any other woman, he would.

"I'm making certain that everything is under control," he said, because…he needed to say something, didn't he.

He needed to explain why he'd sought Beatrice out like this, when all the guests who mattered waited for him at the other end of the house. And a glance at his sister showed that she had a bit of hectic color in her cheeks, and a look in her eyes that usually led to bad decisions, but he supposed that was only to be expected with her friends in the room.

"They look as if they're plotting something," he said.

Beatrice did not have to follow his gaze. "Because they are. They're teenagers. That's their job. I can guarantee you that unfortunate decisions will be made, but the hope is that I can minimize any collateral damage."

"I would think your role is to prevent it."

"My goal for the evening is not to prevent scandalous behavior, Mr. Chiavari," Beatrice said with that serenely patient smile. "But to keep it off the internet. To that end, I've confiscated every single one of their mobiles. I have the staff on high alert. All *you* need to do is concentrate on your party."

Cesare realized in that moment that he'd forgotten all about the party.

Something in him turned over at that. As if it was yet another message he couldn't afford to ignore.

Though he tried anyway.

Later, at the banquet table, he watched Beatrice sit with her usual smile in the midst of a pack of teenagers, managing to keep them at a dull roar, with only hints of high-pitched mirth running through the lot of them like an electric current now and again.

But he must have been staring that way for too long. To his right, Marielle stirred, gazing down the length of the table, and then beaming when she looked back at him. "I'm so looking forward to getting to know your sister, Cesare." She paused. Delicately. "She seems like such a colorful girl."

And Cesare found that he did not care for anyone's critiques of Mattea, save his own. He did not frown at Marielle. Not quite. "My sister has not had an easy time of it."

"What I hope, Cesare," Marielle said, reaching over and putting her hand over his on the tabletop where everyone could see, "is that I might offer myself as some kind of role model for your sister as she moves through these formative years. As we both know, a reputation is a legacy waiting to happen. Sometimes it happens against one's will."

Cesare discovered in that moment that he was not particularly interested in discussing either reputations or legacies when it came to Mattea. And he realized he hadn't thought enough about the fact that any wife he brought home might feel, as Marielle clearly did, that it was her job to instruct Mattea on how to behave.

Everything in him balked.

Because there was only one woman he trusted to keep his sister's best interests at heart. Only one he would allow to chastise her. Only one who he would ever permit to speak to Mattea as if she was simply a girl, instead of *his* sister.

And he was not at all certain that Mattea needed a self-professed role model who he had earlier this evening compared to a light fixture.

"Marielle," Cesare began, pulling his hand out from under hers.

He watched panic flash over her features. Or perhaps it something else, something more like determination.

Either way, Marielle leaned in. And without waiting for any sign from him, she pressed a swift kiss to his mouth.

Then she turned, beaming down the length of the table, and let out a laugh that was nothing short of *peals of joy*, wholly unsuited to the moment.

It made the rest of the guests fall quiet, as he understood then that she'd known it would.

"Cesare and I are getting married!" she cried, clasping her hands to her chest.

And the analytical part of Cesare's brain could not blame her. He had told her he meant to propose, then he hadn't. This was supposed to be a business arrangement. It shouldn't matter in the least that she was the one who had called his bluff here.

Especially when she did it so masterfully, leaking a tear or two and throwing herself into congratulatory hugs and praise on all sides as everyone surged to their feet and clustered around the happy couple.

Making it impossible for him to correct her.

Cesare was aware of friends and acquaintances slapping him on the shoulders, offering him the expected felicitations, but his focus was on the far end of the table. The teenagers looked confused. Mattea looked worryingly stone-faced.

And then, though he knew it would hurt—and did not wish to ask himself why—he found Beatrice.

She appeared to be studying her empty plate with tremendous focus, but as if she could feel the weight of his gaze upon her, she looked up.

And for moment, there was only that.

There was only *them*.

There was an honesty between them, at last. Too late. An acknowledgment. An unspoken certainty that made the pressure in his chest all the worse.

When she finally pulled her gaze away, Cesare found himself bereft.

And more than that, engaged.

CHAPTER SEVEN

BEATRICE WOKE UP early on the morning after the party, because she had a job to do.

It was possible, she thought as she marched through the hushed, quiet house, that the simple fact of that job was how she had managed to make it through the night unscathed.

Well. Not entirely unscathed. Not really.

But at least she knew that the places where she'd taken hits, where the way Cesare had looked at her as if she was the only woman alive while literally in the middle of his own engagement to someone else—were invisible.

If the appearance of invulnerability was all she had, she would take it. And hope it became true. In time.

Because the alternative was that she would have to live like this forever, with her foolish heart crushed flat.

Mattea had looked stunned by Marielle's announcement. Then as crushed as Beatrice felt. Then she had looked Beatrice right in the eye and announced to her friends that she intended to make this party one for the history books.

You do not want that, child, Beatrice had told her.

Unsurprisingly, the girls got silly, fast. When the dancing started, the teenagers started stealing bottles of wine and hiding in unused rooms to chug them down, squealing with laughter when caught. When Beatrice finally herded them up to Mattea's rooms, there was too much music—so loud it was a shock they couldn't hear it in the civilized party below.

The *engagement party*, a voice inside Beatrice had kept on repeating, like a death knell.

The girls had pleaded for internet access and when repeatedly denied, had started playing the kind of shrieking, out-of-control games that led to breaking things—or would have, had Beatrice not been there to quietly remove the most delicate objects from their haphazard range.

And then, later, she had been on hand to quietly dispense cold washcloths for clammy brows and buckets for the girls who had chugged the most contraband wine.

Now it was a clear, bright morning, and she could have them sleep, but Beatrice believed in the power of consequences.

So she rousted the lot of them from their slumber, ignoring all the whining with the ease of her years of practice. She dispensed tablets for headaches, insisted each of the girls drink at least twenty ounces of water, and then made the most sullen group of teenagers in Europe keep her company as she stretched her own legs on an extra-long loop through the vineyards.

Twice.

When they came back to the house, drooping and moaning, she had the kitchens deliver up a proper meal to sop up the excesses of their behavior the night before. She shepherded the girls into showers, and supervised their unnecessary makeup and hair routines, all of which went on for ages. It was past midday when she handed off Mattea's friends, who had only been permitted access for one night, to the waiting SUV that would whisk them off to the airfield.

Beatrice allowed herself not one single moment to concern herself with the night Cesare might have had as an engaged man.

Not one.

When she returned to Mattea's rooms, she found the girl curled up in a ball on her favorite couch in the media room, looking as if she didn't know if she wanted to go to sleep…or maybe cry her eyes out. She was everything that was limp and wan, and Beatrice ignored her entirely.

She bustled around the room instead, tidying everything she could. She threw open curtains throughout the suite, opening the windows and the balcony doors to encourage airflow and light, knowing that sooner or later both would revive Mattea.

And she found herself grateful that she was working today. That she had things to keep her busy. She didn't have time to sit around and think too much about the fact that Cesare had finally, actually, gotten himself engaged.

Engaged. To be *married.*

It was no longer a theoretical possibility. It was no longer something she needed to look up on her mobile every morning. She hadn't bothered today, because she already knew the answer. She'd been there to see it with her own eyes.

She couldn't decide how, exactly, she felt about the fact that it was clear—to her, anyway—that he hadn't wanted it to happen like that. It had been Marielle who'd seized that moment and made her announcement.

Beatrice had waited for the powerful and mighty Cesare Chiavari to correct her...but he hadn't.

Instead, he'd looked at Beatrice. And she'd had the most ridiculous urge to claw her way up that long banquet table—anything to get to him—but she didn't know if her end goal was to save him or to slap him.

What she did know was that she didn't have the standing or the right to do either of those things.

She'd been grateful when the girls had started acting up, because she would rather handle overexcited teenagers forever than dig into how she actually felt, having witnessed the father of her child allow the whole party to congratulate him on his engagement to another woman.

And the night had been so busy containing her charges, then handling their splitting heads and tender stomachs, that she'd happily had no time to herself to curl up in a ball, hold her baby belly the way she wanted to, and daydream about a night in Venice that seemed farther away now than it had ever been.

"I don't understand why you can't just *be still*," Mattea moaned then, reminding Beatrice that she was still here. Doing her job. Not in a position to lapse off into daydreams.

Something else she knew she should be grateful for.

"It does no one any good to get stuck in despair," Beatrice told her, or perhaps she was talking to herself. She kept the bustling going, tidying up every surface that she could find, still as amazed as she always was that packs of girls could make such a mess. "These are called the wages of sin, Mattea. I hope you're enjoying the rich, ripe fruits of the choices you made last night."

"Oh, my *God*," Mattea moaned with all the drama of an entire theater run. "Why can't you just say *I told you so* like a normal person?"

Beatrice almost cackled out a laugh at that, more proof that the emotions she wasn't letting herself feel were all over the place. She bit it back at the last moment. Then she glanced over at her charge, who had gone from curling in a ball into lounging about like a full opera heroine. Complete with one arm over her eyes, awaiting her inevitable tragic end.

"Did you enjoy having your friends here for the night?" Beatrice asked mildly, because there was no point adding oxygen to opera.

Mattea made a noncommittal noise. "I guess."

"They all seem particularly high-spirited. I don't know why they've never darkened the doors of Averell."

That inspired Mattea to sigh and shift to a sitting position. "None of their parents care if they get kicked out of school. It's not like they need to be educated. They'll all get their money at eighteen."

Beatrice sniffed. "Imagine having nothing at all to live for."

"It's the opposite of that. It's just that you get what you're looking for at eighteen, without having to get old and weird and having to go on yoga retreats to find yourself."

"Mattea," Beatrice said, quietly. "I don't how to tell you this in a way that you will understand, because I'm afraid it's the sort of thing you have to grow into. But there's so much life beyond eighteen. So very much. Eighteen is scarcely a memory to hold on to, at my age. It was so long ago. And in the fullness of time, it means so little."

And she knew as she said it that it was breaking her own boundaries, but that was the trouble with today. She felt broken.

Besides, it was possible she needed to hear those words herself.

"Right." Mattea only rolled her eyes. "But I'm

guessing nobody handed you a memorable trust fund. So."

"What I got was much better than that," Beatrice replied, straightening from the bureau she'd been attempting to clean, though she feared the scratches she'd found there might be permanent. "I had no trust fund, you're quite right. What I was given instead was complete and total independence, and I took it."

"Sounds great," Mattea said insincerely, looking and sounding sulky. But Beatrice saw the glint of something else in her eyes. A tiny hint of curiosity she didn't want to show, but couldn't hide. "Can I have my mobile back now?"

Beatrice reached into one of the deep pockets in the smock she was wearing and pulled out the girl's mobile phone, tossing it to her. Mattea missed it and let it clatter to the floor, but then only stared at it where it lay. She didn't even reach for it when the screen lit up, alerting her to a new notification.

"The thing about my friends is that they're not really friends," Mattea said after the screen went dark again. "It's more like whenever one of us got into trouble in the various schools we all went to, the other ones were there to make it worse. And then, later, talk about how funny it all was. But I think… Sometimes I think that a real friend would do the opposite."

Beatrice understood this as the heartfelt confession it was, and so she didn't rush over to Mattea's side. She sat instead on a chair on the opposite side of the room and kept her expression interested—but not *too* interested—so as not to overwhelm this moment of teenage vulnerability.

"It seems to me that there's a difference between friends and fans," she said when it was clear that Mattea could stare at her mobile on the floor forever. "The fact is, Mattea, you're excellent at giving a good performance. I don't mean that as an insult. I watched you do it all year long at Averell. If I had really wanted to punish you, I would have done it with solitary confinement. Because you truly bloom when you have an audience."

"I've had to sit through a lot of therapy," the girl replied with a shrug. "I know it's bad. Seeking approval. People pleasing. Childhood trauma, blah blah blah."

"That's one take on it," Beatrice agreed. "On the other hand, you could also channel that particular urge, because it's something you're good at, into something more positive."

"Like what? Multilevel marketing?"

Beatrice couldn't hold back a laugh then. "I somehow doubt that your future is in tawdry, tiered sales, Mattea. I was thinking something more like acting."

She watched as the girl's face went blank for a moment. Then something soft and deeply emotional took root there, making her look young and sweet and almost wistful.

But in the next moment, all of that was gone, replaced by scorn.

"Because of my mother?" She sat up straighter so she could wrap her arms around her chest, and then hold on tight. "What would make you think I would want to be anything like her?"

"Acting is a noble profession," Beatrice said matter-of-factly. "More than that, it's an art. I might even call it a privilege. To inhabit the skin of others, to truly have the opportunity to walk in their shoes? That doesn't sound like work to me. It sounds like a gift."

Mattea was up and on her feet, then. Beatrice watched in as much amusement as compassion as she began to pace back and forth in the room, protesting this idea that had clearly hit a button for her.

"You don't understand, because you didn't know my mother, but that's the whole problem. No one knew my mother. She couldn't be known. There was nothing there." She shook her head. "She was just… a collection of scenes and bits she'd found along the way so she could make herself into her very own personal Frankenstein."

"By all accounts, your mother was a very accomplished—"

"My mother made a handful of artsy films," Mattea bit off, sounding cold, though her blue eyes were wild. "And then she married into this family. And after that, the only acting she ever did was pretending she was happy."

Beatrice didn't know why that winded her, when she'd never known the woman. She'd only ever seen the same still photographs that everyone else had. She had been shockingly pretty with her sky blue eyes and flaxen blond hair. It was not the least bit surprising to Beatrice that people still wanted to project their imaginations onto a face like that.

"All I'm suggesting is that you might enjoy a bit of theater," she told Mattea now, as the girl continued to pace. "As a way to channel some of the desire for new experiences into more worthy avenues."

"So I can be just like her, is that it?" Mattea asked, her voice rising. "Everybody's favorite when the spotlight is on, but what happens in the dark? What becomes of something so shiny then?"

Once again, Beatrice found herself almost speechless, when she knew she couldn't let that happen. She knew she had an obligation to show up for the girl. No matter how difficult it was for her. This wasn't about her.

It didn't matter that it resonated.

"Mattea," she began again.

"Our mother," came a voice from the door, "should have shined like the beacon she was, for all of her days. It is a tragedy among tragedies that she could not."

And when they both turned toward the sound, Beatrice's jaw wasn't the only one that dropped slightly at the sight of Cesare there in the doorway.

Though for different reasons.

He had been in formal attire last night. He was usually in formal attire, Beatrice thought with some surprise, though she had never really put that together before. Here, in his own home, he preferred bespoke suits—as if he liked to remind himself that he was meant to be an institution, not merely a man.

This afternoon he wore nothing but a pair of visibly soft sweatpants and a gray T-shirt whose sole purpose seemed to be clinging to every single plane of muscle in his chest. Not to mention his ridged abdomen.

Beatrice had the great pleasure and deep agony of knowing exactly what was underneath that stretch of gray, as well as the sweatpants that emphasized his strong thighs and seemed to love the most rampantly male part of him too well.

It took her too long to come to the obvious conclusion that he'd clearly just returned from some kind of workout. But then the silly little fool inside of her was far too quick to wonder if that was because he'd woken up this morning and tried to chase his demons away.

Hopefully, the one he'd agreed to marry last night.

You are delusional, she chided herself. *And for all you know, his fiancée is lovely. Her only sin is not being you.*

Mattea was staring at her brother, with that same mix of too many emotions on her face. But the one that stabbed Beatrice through the heart was hope.

A wild flash of *hope*.

"It is not her fault that she could not stay as bright as she started," Cesare told his sister, his voice and his gaze intent. "There are some men who find beautiful things in this world and wish to possess them. They take them in their hands, they hold them too tight, and then they blame the things themselves when they are crushed."

"Is that what you think?" Mattea's voice was small. "I used to hear my father yelling at her. That her glory days were long past. That she should have been more grateful he was willing to tolerate her in her decline."

Cesare made a low noise. "I'm sorry you heard that. You should not have."

Mattea blew out a breath. "She always said that the best way to make people remember you is to be unforgettable, by any means available. And she could throw parties. She could cause scandals. All I had was school. And my father didn't remember me when I was home. So I thought I might as well...use what I had to remind him."

Cesare was still in the doorway, and the darkly intent look he shot Beatrice made everything in her stand on its head. Then cartwheel all around.

As if he knew her. Or at least, as if she had something to do with him showing up here like this.

She wanted so badly to imagine she had gotten through to him somehow. That whether he remembered her or not, something deep inside him *knew* her all the same.

The way she knew that man he'd shown her in Venice.

The one she persisted in believing was still in him, somewhere.

Right now she didn't have to look very hard.

Soon enough, it wouldn't matter what he remembered or recognized, because nothing that occurred in this house or this family would be her concern any longer. Beatrice needed to find a way to hold on to that.

"I have never forgotten you, Mattea," Cesare told his sister, shifting all of his force and intensity back to her. "I never could. And there's something I should have told you a long time ago. I am not your guardian because your father wanted to get rid of you. I am your guardian because I demanded that he relinquish you to my care. Because I did not think he was doing a very good job."

Beatrice knew she wasn't the only one holding her breath, then. But she was sure that she was the only one who had suggested that he'd been something less than the perfect guardian to his sister. The only one who had wondered if, maybe, he might try being there for her with more than just his money.

She had never felt anything like this. The sheer joy that he had *listened*. And that he was here now, saying these things to a shaken, lost girl who needed desperately to hear these words, straight from him.

"You seemed to like me more when you saw me less, Cesare," Mattea said, with that shattering teenage honesty.

Cesare, to his credit, had the grace to take that hit. To look chagrined, and to let his sister see it.

"I realized last night that I have not explained these things to you," he said, and he did not sound as if he thought that was an excuse. "When I was your age, I was being prepped to run an empire. And the way I made myself memorable was with perfection. Because I could not afford to do anything less. It is possible that I expected you to simply do the same, when you have no empire to run or enemies waiting to see you fall. All you need to do, Mattea, is try not to let anyone take your shine." He inclined his head. "Even me."

His sister looked down, and seemed to remember the night before, and the shenanigans she and her cohort had engaged in. Or perhaps it dawned on her that it was not normal for her brother to make appearances here. "You never come to my rooms. Are you going to send me away again? Because I didn't behave like a proper little princess at your party?"

"Did you not?" And again, Cesare's dark gaze slid to Beatrice and made her throat go tight. While it seemed everything else in her lit on fire. "I will confess, I did not notice."

"I contained it," Beatrice said, shooting for a crisp tone and not quite getting there. "As promised."

She told herself it was a relief when he turned that dark blue gaze back to his sister.

"I realize that I have not discussed with you what will happen when I marry," Cesare said. "I only mentioned that I wished to do so."

"Well," Mattea said, forthrightly, with a resigned sort of shrug. "You were always going to marry someone like that Marielle."

Beatrice would have left the room immediately if she could, because this was none of her business. But Cesare was blocking the door that led toward the exit with that unfairly beautiful body of his. And only she knew she'd gotten to taste every bit of that body, thoroughly. And if she closed her eyes, she could taste him again right now.

And it didn't matter what he knew or didn't know.

What she knew beyond any shadow of a doubt was that she did not want to stand here and listen to a discussion of his fiancée. It was too much. In a summer of entirely too much, this was...*beyond.*

She wasn't sure she could take it.

"What do you mean?" Cesare was asking and not in that quiet, dangerous tone he sometimes used, when he was warning off any follow-up questions. He seemed genuinely interested. "What, precisely, is 'a woman like her'?"

"Like she's made of reflective glass," Mattea said, and she was getting her equilibrium back. It was there in the color that was slowly coming back into her cheeks. Even her tone had returned to its usual dismissiveness. "So she can mirror all that Chiavari legacy stuff you like to go on about. I thought that was why you were getting married in the first place."

Cesare let out a small sound, as if he had taken a hit to the gut, and Beatrice kept her eyes firmly on the floor. She expected him to launch into a defense of his betrothed.

But he didn't.

He didn't, something in her whispered, as if that meant something.

As if it was personal. To Beatrice.

How shameful that she wished it was.

Cesare crossed over to the couch Mattea had vacated. He swiped up the remote control and pointed it at the screen on the far wall. "I have an idea," he said. "Why don't we watch one of the films?"

Mattea reacted as if someone had slapped her. "One of… Our mother's?"

Cesare sat, clicked through a few menus, then patted the cushion beside him. "I am not an actor in any regard, but I have always been very good at negotiations. And what is a negotiation except a kind of performance all its own? If I were you, I would ask myself what gifts our mother left you. Not what stories people tell about her. Even if those people are me."

"People sometimes say I look like her," Mattea said, in a small voice. "They don't say it nicely."

"Because beauty like hers is not a gift," Cesare said, very seriously, holding her gaze in a way that made it clear that he agreed that Mattea resembled her. "It was her curse. People remembered her face, never her. So she thought she had nothing more to offer. But you and I know better, do we not?"

And this time, when he pointed to the cushion beside him, his sister went and sat there next to him. Through one film, then the next.

Beatrice sat through the first one with them, only

because when they had both protested when she'd tried to leave. Almost as if they weren't sure how to be together, she thought. But while they'd watched their mother, she had watched them.

And had wondered if she would have to *actually* bite her tongue to keep herself from asking all the questions she wanted to ask. Like where was Marielle? What had brought Cesare here to make things better with his sister?

Did this mean he no longer needed her to play her headmistress role?

She was dismayed at how sad the prospect of leaving this place made her, when she should have rejoiced that she could go, her secret still safe with her.

During the second movie they screened, she made her way down to the kitchens and sorted out a late afternoon meal for them. The house was quiet, as most of the guests had left in the first part of the day. The servants' quarters were sparsely populated as well, as the bulk of the cleanup had already taken place and many were off having well-deserved personal time. Beatrice carried in a tray of food and slid it onto the table nearest the couch, but then stopped short.

Mattea had fallen asleep, her head on her brother's shoulder. And Cesare was not looking at the screen in front of him, where his mother was riding on a train, looking sadly out of windows streaked with raindrops.

He was looking straight at Beatrice.

"We should find her acting lessons," Beatrice said, though her voice sounded far more fluttery than it should have. She cleared her throat. "If she's even a little bit her mother's daughter, she will be extraordinary."

Cesare only looked at her, his gaze dark, brooding.

"And I really do think that if she has a place to channel that energy, she might find that making trouble holds far less appeal," Beatrice continued, though she was aware that something inside of her had caught fire. It was connected to the way he was looking at her, like a livewire that went deep, and everything inside her seemed to...*spark*.

"Little owl," he said, which made no sense, "I do not wish to speak any further about Mattea."

Beatrice wanted to say something, to do something, because she felt she needed to *do something*—

Especially when he turned, carefully cradling his sister's head as he shifted her body until she could curl up against the back of the couch and sleep on.

And as Beatrice watched—somehow frozen still—he stood.

Then walked toward her, portent in every step.

Or maybe it was simply in her, the pounding of her blood in her veins. The honey in her limbs, the heat sweet and slick between her legs.

He advanced, she fell back, and she didn't realize until too late that it was a tactical misfire. Because she let him back her fully out of the room.

Now Mattea was in the room beside them with the film still playing, Beatrice was in some small salon with no witnesses, and then Cesare was there too, taking up all the air. All the space.

All she could see or hear or breathe.

I remember this, something in her said with great satisfaction—

But she couldn't melt into that. She *couldn't.*

"Mr. Chiavari," she began desperately. "I really think—"

"That is the trouble," Cesare said.

His eyes were so dark, she thought, and he was so close now, and she was not immune. She had tried for so long now, but she was still not immune.

"The trouble?" she asked.

But she was whispering.

"Too much thinking," he said, closing the distance between them until her breath felt like his. Until *she* felt like his, when she knew better.

Cesare studied her face for so long that she thought he might fog up her glasses, but instead he leaned forward, slid his palm over her cheek to hold her face steady, and kissed her.

Finally, he kissed her.

And it made her realize in a searing burst of *thank God* that every dream she'd had about him since Venice was a lie. It was all smoke and mirrors, fuzzy and filtered.

Because the real thing was so much better.

The taste of him was so much wilder, and far more devastating.

Their mouths fit together the way they always had. As if they'd been carved from the same bit of sensation and their lives had been an exercise in finding their way here. Finding their way home.

And she was too aware that her body was different now, and even more his than it had been that night, little though he knew it.

He kissed her again, then again, then he took the kiss deeper, and sensation was so sharp it felt like she was being lacerated by the pleasure—

But he was engaged to another woman. There was no mistake. She had been there.

And Beatrice could not be the kind of person who did this, could she?

I won't, she sobbed within. *I can't.*

She pushed herself away from him, horrified. Deeply horrified.

Though what she was really horrified about, she could admit only deep inside herself, was that she wasn't as horrified as she should have been, and certainly not for the right reasons.

Because he felt like hers. He always had.

Yet he was Cesare Chiavari. And she was a former headmistress teetering on the brink of total disgrace.

And she told herself it wasn't surrender but strategy when she whirled around, wishing she was as nimble as she'd been before she was pregnant, and ran.

CHAPTER EIGHT

THERE WERE TOO many things slamming their way through Cesare, then, none of them gentle. All of them catastrophic.

There was a kind of knowing he didn't want to accept. A recognition—

Yet still, something in him refused it. All of it.

Because what mattered was that he had just proved that he was not the man he'd always believed himself to be. The man he had prided himself on being. The man he had assumed he would always be, so pure and perfect were his intentions and his goals.

It hadn't even been that hard to walk the path he'd chosen. He'd assumed that was a testament to the strength of his character, or perhaps a simple acknowledgment that he was right to place the family legacy above all else.

But now he understood that he had never been tested.

He had never been tempted.

The man he'd imagined he was, honorable and brave, would never have allowed himself to be claimed by one woman the night before, then kiss a different one come the morning. The man he'd been certain he was all these years would never have found himself in such a situation.

He would have proposed to Marielle ages ago. He would have married her by now.

He never would have paid the slightest bit of attention to a round little owl.

Cesare realized that for the first time in the whole of his life, he had no idea who he was.

The headmistress turned and fled. He could hear her feet down the length of the hall, then the door to Mattea's suite slam behind her as she burst through it.

Maybe he should take that as a sign. A call to his better self, to be the better man he'd always imagined he was, before today.

But his blood was so hot inside his body that he thought he might scald himself. His sex was so hard it ached. For some reason, he kept mixing up Beatrice and his lady of Venice—

Something hovered, just there, but he didn't want to accept it.

And before he knew it, he was going after her.

He didn't see her when he made it to the hallway. Remembering one of the little jibes she'd thrown at him, he made his way to the servants' stairs and climbed up them, all the way up to the rooms beneath the eaves.

The afternoon light streamed in from the end of the hall. He expected to encounter other members of his staff, only to belatedly remember that he'd given most of them the rest of the weekend off. He thought he should have been able to hear Beatrice in whatever room was hers, and he stood there, trying to control his own breathing so he could hear hers.

And this might have been his house, but he did not feel right about peering into the private spaces of the people who made this house run. Cesare stood there in the hallway, aware that he was having far too much trouble controlling himself.

It was more evidence that he was lost. That he was not himself. That he had no access to the man racked with need who had taken over his body, his mind, all of him—

Because inside him, still, there was a kind of storm. And he had the sense it hadn't yet hit ground.

A voice inside that sounded a great deal like his memory of his late father whispered, *You do not want that, my son. You know where it leads.*

Maybe it was a good thing that he couldn't find his little owl.

To break the tension—or to find his way back to himself, somehow—Cesare walked down to the window at the end of the long, narrow hallway. It was round and high, and when he looked out at first he saw the same view he always did. Rolling hills, cultivated vineyards, olive groves.

His legacy, arrayed before him like a painting, just as he liked it.

He had gone for a very long run this morning,

after a long and sleepless night, much of which had been spent at a party he wished he hadn't thrown, fielding congratulations that sat heavy on him.

Are you pleased with yourself? he had asked Marielle at the end of the night when he walked her to her chamber, because it had seemed expected. And he was a man who always did what was expected, didn't he?

I will be happy when I am the next Chiavari wife, she had replied, with that same smile. *As we have discussed for a long time now.*

I did not realize that happiness was in the cards, he had replied, without thinking.

When he should have known better. He and Marielle could live a long life together, fully content with each other, but it was predicated on not allowing such unnecessary glimpses behind the curtain.

Had he really believed, for so many years, that a life like that was what he wanted?

And for the first time, he thought he'd seen the real Marielle there, lurking in the bones of her objectively lovely face.

We will create a perfect legacy, she had said, almost sternly. *We will nurture it into something robust that will stand the test of time. What is* happiness *next to that?*

He had turned that question over and over in his head ever since.

It was what had prodded him to run faster and faster on his run, but not because he had come round to Marielle's way of thinking. Or back to what his own thinking had been when he'd started this search for an unobjectionable wife, who would fit into his life like the mirror his sister had accused her of being, with a lack of heat that had seemed like an indictment.

He had thought about his lady of Venice, as ever. He had thought about Beatrice.

But it was his sister who had weighed heaviest in his thoughts.

His sister, who Marielle believed needed a role model. And more, that she was the perfect person for the position. She, a woman who would pretend that he had proposed because she was tired of waiting—and not because she was so taken with him that she couldn't bear another moment apart.

He had run faster and farther, knowing that wherever he ran, it would be on land that was his. That the earth beneath him was his legacy. That it would remain long after he was gone, and that was a contentment that nothing could take away.

And more, that he might not count happiness as a virtue worth pursuing—or he never had—but he wanted something better for Mattea.

She deserved, at the very least, to choose.

Beatrice had been trying to tell him these things all along, hadn't she?

That was what had brought him to her rooms, with dirt from the Chiavari vineyards still on his shoes.

Now he was only regretful that he hadn't gone to her sooner, to speak to her of the mother they'd shared.

Still at the window, he let his gaze drop straight down to the pool area that only family and staff knew about. It was separated from the rest of the house by high walls festooned with flowering vines, and over time it had become almost exclusively the purview of the staff, because Mattea had a marked preference for the eternity pool on the opposite side of the house, set against a stunning view in the distance, some glorious landscaping, and shade. For his part, Cesare always meant to swim, yet usually found himself running instead.

But today, he stood there, transfixed.

Not because of the pool itself, though it was a sweet turquoise invitation in the golden afternoon light. But because he could see his little owl, marching across the flagstones toward the pool as if on one of her missions. She was still fully clothed in her usual drab, unflattering shrouds of clothing, with what looked like an extra smock today. Her enormous glasses were still on her face, and he remembered that he had felt them pressed against his own cheekbones before.

Why should that wash over him like heat?

And there was something about her mouth that was sitting on him strangely, urging him to *think*—

But instead, he watched Beatrice, several stories below, as she took herself to the water's edge. She stood there for a moment, and even from this far away he could sense the tension in her.

Until, fully clothed, she threw herself in.

A different sort of drumming began, deep inside of him.

Because he was perfectly clear what was happening here.

She was washing herself clean. She was washing *him* off.

Cesare did not like it at all.

And he stopped worrying about what kind of man he was.

Everything seemed to go narrow inside his chest, a taut spiral that was made of stone and fire. Without intending to move, he found himself charging down the servants' stair. When he got to the bottom, down in the kitchens, he had no memory at all of whether or not he'd passed anyone on his way down. It was all blank space in that fire within him.

He made his way outside, then into the secret pool area through an ancient door set in the thick walls covered in vines that were older than some American cities. The door opened and closed noiselessly, though he would not have cared if it had scared off half the birds in Tuscany. Cesare strode to the side of the pool, scowling down into the water, at first not able to make sense of what he saw.

It looked like there were shadows, everywhere, floating beneath the water—

But he realized in the next moment that what he

was seeing were those shroud-like clothes of hers, because she was tearing them off under the surface of the pool.

And the very moment he took that in, his gaze was drawn to the stair across the water, where she was rising up like some kind of mermaid from the very depths of his deepest, darkest fantasies.

Beatrice was completely nude.

And her hair… Her hair was no longer caught up in that achingly tight bun on the back of her head. It flowed down, impossibly long, and the water made it seem as dark and as smooth as ink as it poured down her back.

She turned, as if she heard him. As if she could hear that thundering inside his chest, like it really was a drum.

As if she could feel the ache in his sex.

She froze, there on the stair without a stitch of clothing on a body that was nothing short of a celebration of the female form, looking back over one perfect shoulder toward him.

The first thing he thought was, *She's taken off those hideous glasses.*

And then, at last, he recognized her.

He recognized her.

"You…" Cesare breathed.

And that magical miracle of a night in Venice slammed into him, a cascade of heat and longing and need.

Because she was the very same woman. She was

his lady of Venice. She was the woman who had exalted him and ruined him, and he had never been the same.

Now that he knew it, he couldn't understand how he had missed it all this time.

She had lived here, under his roof, and had interacted with him for more than a month and he hadn't known—

Then again, maybe he had.

Maybe his body had always known the thing his mind had not wanted to accept.

Because there was no other explanation for his obsession with a drab little owl who was here to keep Mattea in line, save this.

In his dreams, he had known. His subconscious had recognized what his eyes did not. There were parts of him that had known all along.

She had been haunting him...because she was here. Not a ghost at all, but the woman he dreamed of each and every night.

And he thought that somehow, this must have been fated all along. Destiny, when he had long believed that Chiavaris made their own destiny, by their will and their legacy alone.

It was no wonder he'd been dragging his feet where Marielle was concerned. It made perfect sense that he had been unable, somehow, to give the family ring to the wrong woman.

Because the woman he truly wanted, the one woman he craved, was right here.

"Sei il mio tesoro," he said, almost roughly. *"Sonno pazzo de ti."*

Because she was a treasure to him, and she'd been right here beneath his nose. And he was more than half-mad for her, in whatever form she took.

But as he watched, feeling as if he had been turned into stone, something changed in her gaze. She took a deep breath. He could see the way she straightened her shoulders.

Then she turned all the way around. And his gaze dropped to take in the unmistakable jut of her belly.

The baby she carried.

Mine, something in him roared at once.

And it was as if everything in him shattered into pieces.

He heard a sound, low and animal, and understood that it was that same roar, from a place he hadn't known he carried inside.

Because it was as if he had spent the whole of his life trying to figure out who he was, and now he knew.

Now there was no doubt.

Now he was *himself*, at last.

He made that noise again, and it was like a song. And then he was moving, rounding the edge of the water, and bearing down upon her with intent.

With unmistakable intent.

"Cesare…" she whispered, as if in some kind of apology.

But he did not want words. He had no need for apologies.

He wanted…everything.

It was as simple and as impossible as that, so he kissed her.

Again, and again and again, a slick, hot claiming.

A reminder.

A deep, hot, long-overdue recognition.

He set her away from him, tugged off his own T-shirt, and dressed her in it. It was almost like a dress on her, though her belly made it shorter, and despite that glorious red thing she had worn on the night they'd met, he somehow knew that his lady of Venice who was also Beatrice Higginbotham did not spend a lot of time wearing scandalous, body-baring attire.

It was all for him.

She was all for him.

And Cesare hauled her close, then into his arms, and carried her into the house.

To his bed, at last.

CHAPTER NINE

BEATRICE HAD LOST herself in this dream a thousand times. A soft bed at her back. The glory of Cesare braced over her. That shatteringly intense look on his face that she could feel all over her, within her, as if they were the same.

As if where it counted, they were one.

She'd had this dream again and again and again, but this was different.

This was better, when that should have been impossible.

The sun was gold and red and molten outside the windows, making them both glow. And Beatrice lay there in that very same T-shirt she'd been admiring earlier, wrapped up in the scent of him. Her body was hungry in ways she'd tried so hard to forget, heavy and needy, and this time she wasn't going to wake up bereft and alone.

Best of all, his hands were on her belly. He was frowning in total concentration as he learned the new shape of her, sliding his palms beneath the shirt and over the mound of the baby they'd made.

And every dream she had involved different re-enactments of the night they'd shared in Venice. She had been mining a memory and on some level, she'd imagined she would keep doing it the rest of her life. But this was something else.

This was all new, and better still, they knew each other now.

He knew her name. She knew him.

They had spent weeks together, not a few wondrous hours.

Venice had been like a dream even when it was happening.

This felt like poetry.

Like the passion she'd known was in him all along.

He laid kisses on either side of her navel. His warm palms, hotter by the second, smoothed down the slopes of her bump as he whispered words of praise and adoration in Italian.

Sweet little sonnets all for her, and their baby.

Our baby, she thought, and that was a revelation all its own—and it could not matter, not in this precious moment she had not believed would ever happen, that there were complications hovering there, just outside the bedroom—

Beatrice pushed them aside. Because this belonged to them, and the memory of the night that had changed everything. This was theirs alone, and the future that kicked inside of her, as if the baby recognized its own father.

And somehow, the sweetness of this introduction—

not only of herself to this man who had changed her life, but of this father to the baby he should have been expecting from the start the way she had been—made everything...

More.

The sweeter the things he murmured to the baby, the hotter it was. The more carefully and reverently he touched her, the more restless she became, desperate to wrap her legs around him the way she had in Venice—though she supposed that would not be as easy now.

It might not even be possible in her current shape, but the longing only intensified. The *wanting* only deepened.

She had known he was her baby's father, of course, but Beatrice had never understood until now how all the different things he was to her could twine together.

Brother to his sister. Father to their child. Lover of her dreams, finally in the flesh once more.

He was Cesare, and in some way, she had always considered him hers—even knowing that she couldn't have him.

And maybe this was a dream after all, but maybe this was the one she would never wake up from. Because time seemed to flatten out and turn to honey like the rest of her, like the sky outside, as Cesare crooned to her belly, whispered promises, and pledged himself to their unborn child as if he had wanted nothing more than an unexpected pregnancy all this time.

There was so much emotion inside of her that Beatrice hardly knew how to keep it all inside. She tried. She told herself there were things that needed to stay hers—

She did her best, but it all spilled out anyway.

"I thought you would cast me out," she found herself saying. She pushed herself up on her elbows to look down at him as he crouched there, his hands tracing lazy patterns over her belly and a look of wonder on his face. "That you would call me a gold digger, or something in that vein."

"You would have had to know who I was." He lifted his gaze, a deeper, darker blue than any she had ever seen. "There are many things to discuss, Beatrice, this is clear, but I know full well you had no idea who I was. Any more than I knew you. It is a fact I have regretted ever since."

"Cesare..." she whispered, but not because she had anything particular to say to him. More because she felt a wild, deep joy that she could call him that. Here, now. His name was known to her, *he* was known to her. She could lie back, naked and gloriously pregnant, and still sing it at the top of her voice if she wished.

Yet try as she might, she couldn't keep the complications at bay. There was last night. There was still the very same reason she'd run to that pool and tried to scrub her need for him off her skin. It wasn't that the joy in sharing the baby with him ebbed. She wasn't sure it ever would.

But it was layered with other considerations, whether she liked it or not.

"You asked another woman to marry you," Beatrice made herself say. She made to sit up, to pull away from him, and shook her head when he stopped her. "This is wrong."

"Two things," he said, in that dark and stirring way of his. "First, I did not ask her to marry me. I intended to, months ago, but something held me back." His gaze searched hers. "You, Beatrice. Shuffling around in your headmistress costume, right under my nose. I could not understand why you drew my notice, why I could not look away, why I dreamed of Venice but saw glasses and a tight bun instead." He watched as she took that in, flushing with a pleasure she couldn't make herself contain. She wasn't sure she tried. "And second, you can consider things ended with Marielle from this moment forward."

It was shocking, really, how much she wanted to do just that. "I doubt she will consider it ended, however much *I* might."

"Marielle wants a spotless legacy over which she can reign."

"So do you," Beatrice whispered. "You speak of little else."

"I thought I did." He shook his head, his gaze dropping to her belly. "But you and I, this child we made, this is not spotless and still, it is beautiful."

And Beatrice felt her whole body relax at that, in a way she had not let herself relax since she first knew she was pregnant. And certainly not since she'd come to Italy.

Some part of her had not believed, until now, that it was possible she would be okay.

But he thought it was *beautiful*, this mess they'd made. This miracle.

Cesare looked almost rueful. "I have no doubt that Marielle will be delighted to be released from any connection with me."

Beatrice thought she should argue. That she should insist that they sort out the matter of his engagement now, and it didn't matter to her that it was clear Marielle would not have done the same if their positions were reversed. It wasn't about Marielle. It was about the kind of person Beatrice had always thought *she* was—

But Cesare was moving up the length of her body to settle himself beside her, and his face was so close to hers that he was all she could see.

She forgot anything and everything but this. But him.

At first, after Venice, she'd believed that she would never see him again. And then she had, and that had been worse. Then it had all been a kind of torture, but she had soldiered on because she'd truly believed it would be good for her child.

And because she'd discovered that she cared quite a lot for Mattea, whose behavior she understood so much better now. And, of course, because she liked being near Cesare. She craved it.

Even when he didn't recognize her.

But Beatrice was only flesh and blood, in the end. She was only human. Headmistress Higginbotham was the armor she wore, and she had spent years perfecting it, but the reality was this. A woman lying naked and big with child, in bed with the only man she had ever touched. The only man who had ever touched her. The man she had longed for ever since she'd met him, before she'd known who he was and after.

And it turned out she had precious little strength left to resist him.

She reached over, because she could, and she traced the dark arch of one brow, then the other. She tested the line of his proud nose, his sensual lips. She shivered, imagining the way he could use them on every last inch of her, the way he had in Venice.

The way she knew, somehow, he would again now.

"But I have heard you talk about the kind of life you want," she heard herself say, because there were still sharp little poking things, there in the back of her mind, "and it isn't this, Cesare. It isn't the man who showed up in his sister's room today and healed something in her. I… I can't reconcile the two."

"I will tell you."

He pressed his mouth to her cheek, her jaw. To one corner of her mouth, then the other. He found her temple, then the soft spot between that and the shell of her ear.

"Last night I stood at the bottom of the grand stair while the woman I had carefully selected to be my wife walked toward me. But all I was interested in was you, a woman my would-be bride did not even notice was there." A strand of her hair lay between them, sodden and dark, and he paused to curl it around his index finger with great deliberation. "I excused myself from world leaders and men with great power when I would normally speak with them for hours, so I could watch you hold court over a handful of teenagers. And I resented it when I was forced to take my spot at the head of the table, because I was not interested in the tedious conversations and social mores that awaited me. Because, my little owl, though you may not realize this, very little has interested me since your arrival but you."

"Impossible," Beatrice whispered, though she could feel the way her lips curved. "Surely a man of your stature cannot see over the cliff of his own consequence all the way down to a woman of such humble origins as mine."

"I might not have recognized you, Beatrice," he said in a low, thrilling voice that washed through her and over her and made everything inside her *hum*, "but I see you. Hidden behind glasses you do not need, your hair tamed into submission, and swathes of clothes to hide your shape. Still, I saw you. Still I dreamed of you." He made a kind of growling sound. "It was always you."

She thought there was more there, because hadn't he told her something like that, months ago?

I have never been a man of passion, he had told her when he was deep inside of her, keeping her on the edge of that sweet shattering for what had seemed like a lifetime, *but for you, I would learn it. For you,* mi tesoro, *I would become a creature made only of desire.*

Beatrice hadn't let herself imagine that this could happen. That they could finally be together again. He rolled away to kick off his shoes and pants, then came back. He sat her up, stripping his T-shirt from her body and tossing it aside.

And when he lay back down beside her, there was nothing between them but skin, and she wasn't sure she had any arguments left inside her.

"Beatrice," he said, in that dark, thrilling way of his. "Kiss me, I beg of you."

So she did.

Cesare had kissed her in Mattea's rooms earlier, and again by that pool, but this was different. Because this felt like a sacrament.

And Beatrice was greedy enough to think it ought to be. That this kiss should function like a vow, fusing them together. Especially when he moved over her, making pleased, greedy noises as he filled his hands with her bigger, rounder breasts.

"You are so lush," he told her as if the words were too small to contain what he meant, "so beautiful."

And then he laid her back down in the center of his bed, and worshipped her.

Every inch of her, as if this was their new religion, theirs alone to share.

And he wasn't quiet about it. Cesare was inventive and imaginative and he wanted to let her know about each and every discovery he made as he went, so that by the time he made it over her bump and down into that furrow between her legs, she was trembling, her eyes slick with emotion and need.

For he had stretched her out on the edge of that cliff for a long, long while, and he clearly meant to keep her there.

"You are even more beautiful than I dreamed, then I remembered, my little owl," he told her. "But you will be even more beautiful when you come in my mouth."

And then he kissed her there, too.

He licked into her, devouring her, making her arch up to get more of him. As much as she could. There could never be enough. Every touch made her want more.

One lick, another, a twist of his jaw—and she was in pieces.

The lover she remembered took charge then, sliding his fingers into her soft heat and finding his way inside her. And all the while he licked her, again and again, letting her catch her breath only slightly before throwing her out into bliss once more.

Only when she was sobbing, not sure if it was from pleasure—or if she was pleading, or what she was pleading for—did he crawl up the length of her body, moving her hands away when she would have reached for him.

"I wish to worship you," he told her, very sternly. "And I need for you to let me, Beatrice."

And what could she do but obey.

Cesare lay down beside her and rolled her over him, helping her kneel over him. Then he guided her, lowering her down on top of him while they both watched the thick head of the hungriest part of him sink into her soft heat.

He made a rough, low noise and then he gripped her hips. He looked like every dream she'd ever had, true at last. He gazed up at her with those dark blue eyes gone electric.

And then he used his hands at her hips to lower her onto him, inch by inch.

It was a slow, wild stretching. He was so big, so hot and so hard, and her body ached as it accommodated him—because it felt so good. Because it was scalding hot and so beautiful.

Because it was everything she had told herself she would never have again.

Beatrice already knew how beautifully they fit together, but she remembered, too, how he had murmured praise and wonder in her ear as he'd worked himself inside her that first time. How he'd taken such care with her untried body. How he had eased his way inside, a fraction of an inch at a time, until she had been shuddering all around him—not sure if she was sobbing or singing.

Until he'd reached between them, taken that proud little bit of flesh there between his fingers, and introduced her to herself.

Beatrice could see that Cesare was remembering the same thing now. That miraculous first joining in Venice. It had been a culmination of the magic of their meeting, their dancing, their astonishment of having found each other—

And it had only been the beginning.

Tonight, he eased his grip just slightly, though his jaw was tight and his gaze narrow. She could see the faint tremor in him as he held himself in check, his control its own wonder. And she didn't waste the opportunity. She rocked a bit as she straddled him, experimenting with moving one way and another, expecting to feel strange and unwieldy in this new body of hers that kept changing by the day.

But she only felt more beautiful.

And she felt him *more*.

"I would have said that there was no way that you could be more beautiful to me, *mi tesoro*," he told her, his voice hoarse with awe and wonder and that driving need that had its teeth sunk in her, too. "But you have proved me wrong."

"I couldn't believe you didn't know who I was,"

she told him, looking down so their gazes could be as locked together as the rest of them.

And, however disapproving she might have attempted to sound, it all trailed off into a sigh as he smoothed his hands up higher. Then began to tease her breasts, finding them significantly more sensitive than they'd been before.

Just like the rest of her.

"You will forgive me," he said.

"Will I?"

Cesare's eyes were on hers, and he moved his hands again, back down to her hips until he was moving her, too. Raising her, lowering her, and it was like sunburst, like fire.

It was the whole world, and she'd spent a lot of time and effort convincing herself that nothing could be this good. That she'd made that up. That she'd been making excuses for how she'd behaved in Venice, so unlike herself. And how she hadn't even bothered with protection. And all the other things she'd failed to do that night, like guard her feelings, her dreams, her heart—

But this was a revelation all over again.

Her head tipped back of its own accord. Her toes curled.

She had to brace herself on his chiseled chest with her palms as he lifted her up, then slid her all the way back down the hard length of him.

So slow.

So deliberate.

And so good it should have been illegal. It shouldn't have been *allowed*.

Beatrice started to shake all over again, simply because this was happening again. When she'd been so sure that anything that fierce and that glorious could only occur once in a lifetime, on one magical night, to be dreamed of ever after—

But then she was shaking all over again, falling apart, hurtling off of that cliff.

She heard him laugh, and knew that he wasn't going to stop. That this wasn't a dream.

That this was real, and even better than before, and she would be lucky if she survived the intensity of it this time.

In that moment, she wasn't sure she cared.

He gave her no quarter. There was no time to rest, no time to catch her breath.

She fell off of that cliff, but he kept bringing her back and bringing her back until she didn't think she was holding herself up anymore. Cesare was the one who was holding them both there, maintaining that perfect rhythm.

That thrust and parry that made them new every time.

Beatrice couldn't count the number of times she'd broken apart. She lost track of anything and everything but this, this wild communion, this twining of far more than simply their bodies.

Because it really was sacred, this thing between them. This riot of light and color, fire and need.

When she felt him lose track of that rhythm, when his pace broke down and his thrusts became jerky and mad, she held on tight. As best she could.

And when he roared out his pleasure, she felt it from the inside out, and hurtled off into all the light and heat beside him.

It was dark outside the windows when she came back to herself.

She discovered that she was lying on her side, and he was at her back, his arm slung over her with his hand resting on the baby.

It brought home the fact that this wasn't a dream, because all of her dreams had been renditions of that night in Venice. A beautiful night, but only the one night.

She hadn't been pregnant then.

If she was honest, it had never occurred to her that he would accept her pregnancy so easily now. She'd assumed she'd never have the opportunity to tell him about it and if she did, he'd reject the possibility the baby was his without proof. Wasn't that what men like him did in situations like these?

"Don't you want a barrage of tests?" she asked into the dark room. "Don't men in your exalted position insist on establishing paternity, as a matter of course?"

She felt a new sort of shaking and realized he was laughing. That she could *feel* him laughing, just there behind her.

And this was the man she remembered. Not the

Cesare Chiavari she'd met here, brooding and tightly wound and in danger of flying apart at any moment. This was the man she'd remembered all these months, with that voice like a simmering fire and a certain languid confidence that moved through her bones like molten gold.

"The lawyers will demand it," he said, sounding lazy in her ear.

"But you're not concerned."

"Should I be?"

Beatrice felt the faintest brush of irritation, then, though she couldn't have said why. She wasn't sure it made sense. She looked back over her shoulder, shoving her still-damp hair out of the way.

"You could have had a thousand lovers since that night in Venice," she said, though that was the last topic she wanted to discuss. Still, it was realistic, and surely she should cling to such things now, no matter how far removed from *reality* she might feel at the moment. It would help with any whiplash on the other side of this. She hadn't liked that much when she'd experienced it—first when she'd discovered she was pregnant. And again when she'd recognized him instantly, and he had not known who she was. Maybe she could mitigate it. "I assume you have."

"I have not." Cesare moved then, rolling her over so she was more on her back and he could prop himself above her. Once again, he found a thick strand of her hair and played with it, as if looking for hints of red in the dark mass of it. They glinted, as if it at his command, in the soft light from fixtures he must have switched on without her noticing. "I told myself it was because I should not expect an innocent wife if I was not willing to curtail my own activities. But the truth of it, Beatrice, is that I wanted only you."

And she wanted nothing more than to melt into that. Into him.

But this time around she had a child to think of. This time around she needed to protect the both of them.

"How convenient for you that I walked into your palatial home, then," she said, and she could hear that touch of asperity in her voice. She could feel it crashing around inside her.

But he didn't seem to notice. "I have already had my staff reach out to Marielle," he told her. "She was already told that she was not to make any broader announcements, and now she has been made aware that there will be no announcements made at all. I am told she took the news with only a sigh."

Beatrice flinched a bit at that, but could not keep herself from touching him. She traced her finger along the edge of one of his pectoral muscles, then let it go where it would, finding its way along those spectacular abdominal ridges that had haunted her for months now.

"Maybe all she really needs is someone to love her for her," she said but he did not reply.

And that felt like a warning. Beatrice knew she should heed it.

Then again, he'd seen who she was. He'd been inside her, again. He had even accepted the baby. Why should she imagine that this was all happening a little too easily? A little too quickly?

Maybe, she told herself, *you're simply unfamiliar with getting what you really want. It's never happened before.*

Here in his bed, with her hands on his beautiful body, wrapped up with him as if they'd never let go, she could finally admit that he was what she'd wanted all along.

That night in Venice had changed her, profoundly.

She had only been pretending otherwise because she had to. Because she could not say, *I fell in love with a stranger during a one-night stand and I will never be whole again without him,* not even to herself.

"The girls gave me a makeover," she told him now, almost shyly. "They were being funny, obviously. It was a bit of a lark to dress up the headmistress and dare her to go out like that, looking like a total stranger. It never occurred to me that I would do more than have a glass of wine somewhere and let myself be anonymous for an hour or so, then return."

If there were warning signs here, she didn't see them as he shifted, pulling his fingers through the length of her hair, as if testing its weight, its luster.

"I was in Venice for business," he replied after a moment or two. "I had decided at the dawn of the new year that it was time I took the next steps, and

I was certain that I had found an acceptable woman who fit my criteria. Everything was as it was meant to be. And then, there you were. You set all of my good intentions on fire."

She searched his face and what she saw was that same intensity. She remembered it. She'd seen it here, too.

It was part of this thing that always burned inside her, and in him too.

"At first I was glad I did not know your name," she whispered, a new confession. "That made it seem not quite real. Like a dream. I thought that night was a secret I would keep forever. But I missed a period. Then another. And by the time I took a test, it could only tell me what I already knew."

"I looked for you," he told her gruffly, in that same hushed manner, as if this bed of his was a confessional they shared. "I woke up, you were gone, and I could not accept it. I looked for you everywhere that following morning. But no one had seen a ravishing woman, dressed in red, a siren to make men run ashore at the slightest glance. It did not occur to me that she was a costume you had worn."

"I didn't look at a picture of you before I came here," she said, with sudden urgency. "It didn't occur to me that Mattea Descoteaux could have any connection to that man or that night. If I'd known it was you I would never have come like this. I had imagined I would go to Venice once the baby was born, and look for you then."

"But you are here now, little owl."

Cesare kissed her then, long and deep and slow.

And she forgot the other things she might have said, because the kiss caught fire.

This time, he had her brace herself on her hands and knees as he took her from behind, holding her hair in one hand like a rope, so he could find her mouth when she looked back. When he encouraged her to look back and find him.

It was possible that she might have lost a bit of consciousness, there, when he reached beneath her legs and found the center of her need, then pinched it.

Or maybe it was simply that there was a kind of starry sky within her that only he could find.

Over and over again.

And Beatrice fought to find her breath again, Cesare stretched out like a god beside her, and thought, *This is all much more than I ever believed I would have. It's enough. It's more than enough.*

Because it should have been.

But the truth was that she felt like crying.

He rolled out of bed and then hoisted her up in his arms again, carrying her off into his shower to wash them both clean, making them both smell like him.

And maybe she did cry as he used his hands between her legs to make her fall apart once more.

Maybe she sobbed, riding his hand and kissing him like she would never see him again, while heat and steam billowed all around them.

Afterward, he pulled his T-shirt and sweats back

on again. Then he took more time than was strictly necessary to help her into a robe, until she was flushed and perilously close to *giggly*.

So close that she almost pulled him close and whispered those words that were heavier on her tongue by the moment—

But she didn't.

Cesare had been so quick to accept all of this, but he'd never mentioned love.

And Beatrice could not raise her baby without love. She wouldn't. It was the one gift her parents had left her, the greatest inheritance imaginable. And for her, it was a simple thing, there beneath the role she'd played here while she'd waited for him to recognize her.

There had never been another man in her life. There never would be.

She had accepted that a long time ago, never imagining she would see him again. He was it for her.

But though she was brave in so many ways, because she'd had to be, Beatrice could not bring herself to tell him. To say the words that would make her feelings clear.

He walked her back to her attic room, as if this was some kind of date. He stood outside the door to her little room. He looked down at her, and ran the back of his fingers down the side of her face.

Beatrice thought, *This can be enough. I can make this enough.*

And when he bent to take her mouth with his,

sending all those stars and all that molten light spinning through her, she believed she could do it.

She truly believed she could.

But then there was a soft, strangled noise from farther down the hall, and he lifted his head.

And when they turned, Mattea was standing there at the top of the stairs, looking pale and shocked, and worse still, terribly betrayed.

"This was about him," she whispered, her wounded gaze on Beatrice. "This was all about him, wasn't it? It was never about me at all."

"I came here for you," Beatrice managed to say, because that was true.

"Mattea," Cesare began.

But his sister turned that same deeply betrayed expression on him. "You don't care about me at all. You're just as bad as the rest of them. Worse, because they never pretended." She pulled in a ragged breath. "I hate you both."

And then Mattea turned toward the stairs again, and ran for them, her feet like a drum as she raced down toward the bottom of the house.

CHAPTER TEN

LATER, CESARE WOULD castigate himself for a great many things but chief among them that his first response was astonishment.

He froze.

He and Beatrice stared at each other.

"You must go after her," Beatrice said huskily. Shakily.

And he didn't know why he needed her to tell him that. It was as if he didn't know how to behave in the face of that much anguish, but then it didn't matter.

He tore down the stairs, trying to anticipate where his sister would go.

His second bad decision was assuming that she would go to her rooms and barricade herself inside, as she had done on other occasions. He got down the stairs and across the house in record time, but she wasn't there.

And by the time he made it outside and around the front of the house, it was too late.

His sister, who'd long had an affinity for vehicles she was too young to drive, had helped herself to one of the groundskeeper's carts, leaving nothing behind but a cloud of dust.

She was headed for the vineyards. And likely the hills and winding roads that would lead to tiny, medieval villages, and, eventually, Firenze.

He called for the keys to one of the SUVs and followed.

Up one hill, down another, and Mattea knew he was following her. She kept trying to go faster, and when that failed, she began to drive more and more recklessly, as if she thought she could shake him off her tail that way.

Cesare was beginning to wonder if he should fall back, so she would stop the wild stunts with a cart that was not built for such maneuvers—

But then it happened.

Mattea tried to take a sudden turn, too quickly. And Cesare watched in horror as the cart hit stone in the makeshift roadway, launched into the air, and threw his sister free, face-first, into the dirt.

And when he ran to her, she did not wake.

Everything after that seemed like a greasy, slick wheel of adrenaline and self-loathing. Cesare gathered her up as best he could, fully aware that choosing to do that was a risk itself, as he was no doctor and he could not be sure she had not damaged her neck.

But he did it anyway, laying her in his vehicle and calling in for help as he drove back to the house.

Like a maniac.

Then there was the rush to get Mattea up to her rooms again, to lay her out carefully on her bed, as they waited for the doctor he'd sent for to arrive. He had sent his helicopter.

"You must step back and let me look at her," Beatrice said, sounding unnaturally calm to his ears. His blood was so loud in his ears he could hardly bear it, but he let her push through, remembering that she had cared for a great number of students in her time.

That she was not the problem here. He was, just as Mattea had accused him.

"She is breathing. Her pulse is weak, but there." Beatrice frowned up at him. "There is no blood. No broken bones, as far as I can tell."

He could not bring himself to hope. Or even respond.

Cesare knew he would never forget standing by his sister's bed, wondering how exactly he had let this happen. He, who had always had a plan. He, who had been merciless in the execution of that plan across the years.

He, who had prided himself on his perfection.

More than that, he had looked down on those— including his sister—who could not live up to his expectations of a perfect, blameless existence and it was all for nothing. It was all a lie. Some foolishness he'd told himself to prop up his own ego.

Because the truth was that he was a man without control who'd had a one-night stand in Venice. Without protection. And now had a broken engagement, whether he had done the proposing or not. He was about to have a baby out of wedlock with a woman he might find fascinating, but he knew full well his own father would consider her beneath him. Because deep down, wasn't that where Vittorio's fury at Cesare's mother come from? He had believed that an actress was beneath him, and was therefore furious that he could not control her as he felt was his due.

And none of that mattered, because he'd only had one true responsibility in all of that, and it was to keep his sister safe.

He'd thought that taking her away from her useless father had achieved that, but it hadn't.

Cesare had failed in the only way that could ever matter. She was hurt. It was his fault.

He could not bear to imagine all the ways he would fail Beatrice and his own child too.

When the medical team arrived, they were thorough. When they were done examining Mattea, making certain that her minor cuts and bruises were attended to and that any potential for serious injury was explored, they delivered the verdict.

Their expectation was that she would be fine.

Though they were going to have to wait for her to wake up to be certain.

"Leave us," Cesare muttered, because he could not allow himself to feel relief. Not until she woke up and they knew for certain. "Thank you."

And though he'd meant that all the staff should

step out, he was somehow unsurprised that Beatrice did not obey.

"I wish to be alone with my sister," he said gruffly.

She didn't even look at him. "No."

He glared at her, and that felt better. It was someone to blame, and he liked that.

But Beatrice only swallowed, hard, her eyes on Mattea, and he couldn't blame her for anything. "She was very clear, Cesare. She felt both of us betrayed her. I'm not leaving her side again. Not until she wakes up."

Cesare found himself pacing, and he ran his hands through his hair as he moved. "This is my fault. I have always known what is required of me and I should not have lost sight of it. I should never have allowed myself to lose sight of it. Of her."

And he could admit, when Beatrice did not react the way he expected her to, that he was spoiling for a fight. That he really did want to put this at her door, when he knew better. Pretending that she was the problem when he knew it was him was just weakness.

His weakness.

He was the one who had leaned in, back in that *vineria*. He was the one who'd asked her to dance. He had extended the invitation to her to join him in his hotel.

If there was any fault here, it was his.

It was always and ever his.

"When she wakes," he said then, in a voice that did not quite feel like his. It was too precarious. Too uncertain and rough. "I will make absolutely certain that she wants for nothing. That her every need will be met, always. That there is never any—"

"I have an idea," Beatrice interrupted him. He stopped, because he was so seldomly interrupted that he was not certain how one was meant to behave. And she aimed that steady gaze of hers straight into him. "Why don't you try loving your sister? Why don't you start a new legacy with that? How about, when she wakes up, you hug her and say it? *I love you.* See? It's that simple."

But if it was simple, it would not feel like a tectonic crisis, deep within him.

"You forget yourself," he managed to say. "I will not deny there's a passion between us, Beatrice, but you know nothing of this world. It is the world that Mattea and I live in, and always have, and believe me when I tell you I know it well. I do not need childish advice—"

"Childish?" Beatrice threw that word right back at him, her voice rising. Quite as if she was shouting at him. *Shouting.* At *him.* "I'm not the one who had a night like we did in Venice and then decided that a great idea would be to go out and get engaged to another woman. I'm not the one who failed to recognize the other thanks to a different hairstyle and a pair of glasses. How is it possible, Cesare, that a person can be as obviously intelligent and powerful as you are, and yet so very dumb?"

He thought that something in him…exploded. He

felt it, shattered pieces everywhere, and it wasn't as simple as temper. He knew how to deal with that. He'd learned, long ago, to shove it down, to keep it out of sight, to make sure he did not lapse off into jealous rages like his father.

But he was in pieces all the same.

"I was raised by two people who talked all the time about the love they shared when they were in public," he found himself thundering back at Beatrice, across his sister's still form. "And yet at home they were toxic. It was poison."

"People aren't perfect, Cesare," Beatrice threw back at him. "Not a single one ever has been nor ever will be. People are messy. They make mistakes. They hurt each other, and they can't always fix it. They seek forgiveness, and they don't always get it. The most you can hope for is to love the people that you love, as hard as you can and as best as you can, because that's the only thing in this world that you can be sure of."

"Beatrice." And her name came out of his mouth like a plea. "I can give you anything you desire. We will make more children, as many as you like. If what you truly want is a family, I will give you one. But do not speak to me of love. Ever."

And she looked crushed, then. As if she was the one who'd been tossed out of a cart like that, breakable and so fragile, then thrown face-first into the dirt.

That image broke something in him.

But if there was a way to repair it, he didn't know

it. He had the terrible notion that all of his wealth
and all of his power could do absolutely nothing at
all to fix this.

Why don't you try loving? she had asked him.

Beatrice, his unflappable, indomitable headmistress, was shaking now. There on the other side of
his sister's bed, she shook, and he had done this. He
had delivered that wound.

Cesare had never wanted to go to her more. The
pull to her was so intense he thought it was possible
it would cut him in half—

But then, the real tragedy was that he lived. He
took a breath, and nothing was better. Another, and
still she only stared back at him. One more, and his
sister stayed still, while Beatrice waited for him to
be the man he wasn't.

Cesare could not seem to make himself move. And
Beatrice's gaze grew more and more haunted as she
looked back at him.

This was how a vibrant creature like his mother,
capable of lighting up a screen with her smile—not
to mention every room she'd ever walked into—became so small. It happened over time. One disap-
pointment after the next, each and every one of them
delivered by the men she wanted to trust.

He opened his mouth to tell her this, but he couldn't
make his throat work. He slashed a hand through
the air instead, but it did not convey the message he
wanted. It did not warn Beatrice off.

All it did was change that look in her eyes to
something worse. It looked like compassion.

"I can't keep you from hurting your sister," she said quietly. "All she wants from you is what you gave her today. Just love her, Cesare. Spend time with her, like she matters. That's all she needs. That's all anyone needs. Love, time, and hope that there will be more of both."

"I can give you anything in the world," he managed to get out, his voice the faintest scrape of sound. "But I can't promise you that."

"You don't want to," she corrected him. Cesare watched as she stood a little straighter. He could see her throat move. "But you need to understand that I won't let you do this to my baby."

That hit him like a blow. "Both of you will be cared for. Always. How can you doubt this?"

Beatrice's eyes took on a light Cesare did not like at all. "I don't want care. I had *care*, Cesare. I even had decent care, which is more than many people in my position could say. But I want love. And for this baby? I demand it."

Her own words seemed to shock her. She drew in a breath as if she hadn't quite intended to say that.

Cesare could only look back at her, stricken.

But she wasn't done. "I want love," she said again. "And if you can't give it, I want you to leave us alone. I want a real family, Cesare. I refuse to give my child anything less. This baby will know only love at home, all its life. I don't think that's too much to ask."

And he wanted to tell her whatever it took to make her stay, but he couldn't. He couldn't make his throat work. His sister still lay so still in that bed, and he was responsible for that, too. On the very day he had tried to tell her that he loved her as much as he was able. And now the mother of his child was standing before him, asking him for things he could not give.

It was all a mess. It was *his* mess. But he could see no way out of it.

Across from him, Beatrice lowered her gaze. She'd pulled on clothes, but left off the glasses. Her hair was swept back into a bun, but this one was far looser. It was soft, with tendrils that fell out and framed her face. It suited her far more.

In the midst of all of this, it felt like a gift.

Maybe that was why, when she turned and headed for the door with something close to her usual determined stride, he let his eyes fall shut. He let his head go back.

And somehow, though his throat was tight, he got out one single word.

"Don't."

And when he didn't hear her open the door, he forced himself, with everything he had inside, to get out one more. The one that mattered most, and one he rarely uttered.

Not when it could only be what it was. Cesare Chiavari, begging.

He almost thought he wouldn't manage it, but he did.

For her, he managed to eke it out. *"Please."*

CHAPTER ELEVEN

BEATRICE WAS NO stranger to heartache.

But this was different.

Her parents had not wanted to leave her. If they could have lived, they would have. They had not *chosen* the accident that had taken them away from her.

Cesare was choosing this. He was *doing* this.

She had barely accepted that she was in love with him, and already, he was tearing her heart out. The worst part was, she knew him well enough by now to know that it was not something he would do lightly.

He truly, honestly believed what he said. That love was toxic. A poison.

That she could stay, but that he would never love her.

He wouldn't even try.

There was nothing she wanted less than to walk away from him, not now that they'd found their way back to each other, but how could she do anything else?

She turned back to look at him. "Try to understand. My parents died when I was young. And the rest of my childhood wasn't easy, but I always, always knew that they'd loved me. It made a difference." Beatrice pulled in a shaky breath. "There were other children in care who didn't have that, but I did. It was like…a candle in a dark night. You might think that doesn't matter, but if you do, it's because you've never had to look around for that kind of hope."

"Don't think that when I say love is not on the table that that means it will be…" But he couldn't finish that, whatever gritty thing he'd tried to say. He tried again. "Beatrice… You know you wrecked me that night in Venice. You must know this."

That jolted straight through her. It was the way he was looking at her now, with that wreckage right there in his dark blue gaze. She felt it wash over her, making her breath come too hard, too fast.

And she knew it would be too easy to give in, to back down. Because she wanted whatever she could get of him—the fact she'd stayed here all summer proved that. But her hair was down now. The truth was out.

Beatrice didn't think she could pretend again.

There was a very real chance that if she tried, it would kill her.

"I looked for you and I looked for you, but you were nowhere to be found," Cesare was saying. And I am not a man who does not get what I want. That is not who I am. But I could not find you."

He was still by the side of the bed, but he had turned toward the door. And he looked different than she'd ever seen him. It was that starkness on his face. As if he'd been stripped down to his elements and what was left was what she saw now, a man haunted.

As if grief lived in him now, too.

Because it had come so close today. She thought she understood. It wasn't his father, who had been so old. It wasn't his mother, whose choices he openly questioned. It was his sister, a fifteen-year-old who should have a whole life in front of her, but had nearly seen that snatched away.

And he had watched it happen, knowing that he was the reason she had jumped in that cart in the first place.

"I knew I had to let you go," Cesare was saying, stark and serious. "But I couldn't. I dreamed of you every night, though I knew that was not realistic. I knew there was no moving forward with a dream. And you might not think much of the Chiavari legacy, but I was raised to believe it was the only thing that mattered." He shook his head. "I have made sure that it's the only thing that can ever matter."

"You matter, Cesare," Beatrice whispered. She pointed at the bed. "She matters." Then she put her hand back on her belly. "And this child matters. That's your legacy. Don't you see that?"

He lifted up a hand, as if he intended to order her to stop. But he didn't.

"I went through the motions, Beatrice. This is what I'm trying to tell you. I did all the right things.

I followed the plan my father laid out for me before he died. I—"

"Why?" Beatrice asked baldly. "He sounds like he should have sorted himself out before he dispensed advice to others."

And for a moment, she thought she'd gone too far. Cesare looked as if he didn't know if he would collapse beneath the indignity of her remark—or if it might have left a mortal wound.

But he pushed on. "If I could not have the woman who made me think that passion was possible. If I could not find the woman who had torn apart the carefully sewn-up world that I'd been living in for so long, then why not a woman who might as well have been a settee? A dresser? That is all the thought and emotion I put into the question of my marriage. I want you to know that."

Beatrice realized then that she was holding her breath. And even when she told herself to breathe, she wasn't sure she was capable of actually *doing* it.

"And then you arrived." He shook his head, and she thought he looked one part disbelief, another part wonder, but no little bit of temper in between. "This…absurd woman, marching around my family's ancestral seat, issuing orders and dressed like an angry little owl."

"An owl," she repeated. "You keep saying that."

"It's the glasses," he muttered. "I hate them. I want to bronze them. And I, who have never been seen in the company of a woman not held to be among the most beautiful in the world, found myself in pieces over a little round owl profoundly lacking in every possible way. The headmistress who was here to discipline my sister, but appeared to have censure aplenty for me, too." He ran an agitated hand through his hair. "I don't think you can possibly understand how egregious this was. This obsession. This preoccupation with the woman who I should never have even noticed was here."

"How marvelously tender," she snapped at him. "I am all aflutter, Cesare. Truly."

"Why does that not offend me? No one speaks to me as you do, Beatrice. No one except my surly, impossible sister, who everyone assures me will grow out of it once she is old enough to know better, and yet you certainly have not done so."

"The thing about children, Cesare, is that they do not suffer fools until we teach them that they must." Beatrice was still frowning at him. "Maybe that is something you should sit with for a while."

"I don't need to sit with it," he threw back at her, his voice rising in a deeply imperfect, un-Cesare manner. Almost as if he couldn't control himself. "I am Cesare Chiavari. Great men tremble when I enter a room. Women beg for a scrap of my attention. And *you*— You live in my home. You never seek out my company, I must demand it. You dress to hide your beauty and you want nothing to do with me and my obsession with you grows by the moment."

"Cesare," she began, but he ignored her.

"I thought that never being able to find my lady of Venice was the worst thing that could happen. But living without you, thinking that I would never find you, was tolerable only because I came to believe that nothing could possibly be as good as I remembered it being that night." He shook his head. "But once again, Beatrice, you defy me."

"Because it's better," she whispered. "It's so much better now."

They still stood in their respective places, Beatrice frozen by the door and Cesare next to the bed, as if he could not bring himself to step away from Mattea's prone form. As if something held them in place like two strong hands, holding them apart but not allowing Beatrice to end this by walking out the door.

"I can't bear it if you leave me again," he told her then, gruff and low. "And I want all of you. I want my child. I want you, as my wife. My lover. And everything between. And I don't know how to reconcile this with who I have been, who I have wanted to be for the whole of my life. But Beatrice, I look at you and I do not see the point of my duty. Not if it means losing the only woman who I have ever dreamed about—"

"Oh, my *God*," came a sulky, scratchy, deeply disgusted teenage voice from the depths of the bed, and Beatrice felt the tears hovering at the back of her eyes spill over, because she had never heard anything more beautiful. Better yet Mattea's eyes were open. She was already scowling, clearly cranky and out of sorts, and she was glaring at her brother. It was glorious. "You're obviously in love with her, Cesare. And you are *rude*. Why are you *shouting* like this when I'm obviously *dying*?"

"You're not dying," Beatrice whispered, and she didn't care if Mattea could see the tears as she moved toward the bed. She didn't care if Cesare could, too. "You're not dying, child. Thank goodness, you're not dying, because I couldn't bear to lose you. You have to know that I was always here for you first. Always. But I do think you're going to have a terrible headache."

"That's so unfair," Mattea moaned.

And when Beatrice came over to the bed, Cesare met her at the foot. He drew her close, so that the pair of them were looking at his sister. He gazed down at Beatrice. Then he reached over and ran his thumb below one eye, then the other, collecting moisture as he went.

"I think I'm in love with you, little owl," he said quietly, and Beatrice felt her heart seem to quiver behind her ribs. He looked over at his sister. "And I have always adored you, since you were red and squalling and tiny. I'm sorry I made you doubt this for even a moment."

Mattea didn't look remotely shivery. She made a face at her brother, every bit of her alive with disdain.

"Don't *think* you love her," she told him, filled with the contempt that only a teenage girl could manage. "Or me. Just...*love*."

And so, not always easily or gracefully, but always deliberately, Cesare did.

CHAPTER TWELVE

WHEN MATTEA WAS fully recovered, they started to take their morning walks as a trio, and Beatrice forced—she liked to claim she *encouraged*—brother and sister alike to discuss their history, and their feelings, in a way they never had before.

"I hate this," Mattea complained.

"As do I," Cesare agreed.

Beatrice, in headmistress mode, only smiled. "Excellent. We'll make it a family tradition."

They found a prestigious acting camp in the States and Mattea, grumbling all the way, allowed them to pretend to bully her into going. She assured them that the whole thing was dumb and she would hate it, but when it came time to come home after the agreed-upon week, she stayed. For the rest of the summer.

A summer during which there was much speculation in the press about the engagement that wasn't, until Marielle ended it by marrying a minor royal, and even the gossips moved on. A summer, hot and sweet and long, that allowed Beatrice to make amends with the staff who thought she'd infiltrated their ranks to get to the master. Something she insisted was necessary, despite Mrs. Morse's support, though Cesare disagreed.

But he had nothing to argue about. For the first time in his life, he was simply *alive*. He took Beatrice to his bed at night, he loved her with all the passion he had inside him, and he woke up with her every morning.

"If this is an obsession," Beatrice liked to whisper when he was deep inside her, making them both grown, "at least we share it."

They saw the doctors together, took all the tests his attorneys required, and discovered they were having a little boy.

"I do not want to raise a son the way I was raised," Cesare confessed one night, out on the terrace where the setting sun bathed him in gold. "I could not bear it."

"Then we will find another way," Beatrice agreed at once.

One night as the summer came to a close, they sat with his father's letter and Cesare read it to her, point by point. And they agreed that a man could be imperfect and still deliver good advice—but also that it was not necessary to take that advice as gospel.

And so Cesare carefully folded up the letter, tucked it back in its old envelope, and secured it behind the portrait of his father that hung in the gallery. Where he could find it again if he needed it.

But he didn't think he would.

Mattea returned from her acting camp bright and happy. And when it was time for her to go back to school, she took Beatrice aside, and confessed that she didn't know how to go back to a place like Averell and *not* be the troublemaker she'd been before.

"It will be your best role yet," Beatrice told her.

And somehow, Cesare knew that his sister was going to find her feet. And very likely the stage lights, too.

In September, when Mattea was back in school and already involved with her first theater production, he took Beatrice back to Venice.

This time, they both stayed in the private hotel that he had bought in the meantime, so that it could always be theirs when they wanted it. They walked along the canals, held each other close in the piazzas, and she took great pleasure in tossing coins into this fountain and that.

"So we will always return to the people and the places we love," she told him.

And one night, as he danced with her to the sound of a street musician's instrument on a bridge in this city of sighs and wonder, he stepped back. He got down on one knee, held her gaze, and placed his grandmother's ring on the only hand where it could ever belong.

"Please," he said, a word he was getting better at all the time. "My little owl, *mi tesoro*, I love you with all that I am. Will you marry me?"

She did, with none of the fuss or pomp that he

had previously imagined his wedding would require. They did it quietly with the village priest and a trip to the estate's ancient chapel, a beaming Mrs. Morse and Amelia and Mattea as witnesses.

Then they celebrated by walking back through the fields in the vineyards, toward the grand old house that was, he finally realized, just a house without these people he loved. Just a place.

They were the heart, and they made his beat.

Because Beatrice did not simply teach him how to love, she insisted upon it. She loved him back and she told him so all the time.

And for every step he took her closer and closer to the kind of love he thought his wife deserved, he dedicated himself that much more fully to expanding her imagination when it came to the things they could do between them. He did love to watch her eyes go wide.

He also gave her the great big family she'd always wanted.

There was Mattea, who was not their daughter but who they loved as if she could be nothing else. Their son was born that first fall, dark-haired and golden-eyed, like a cannon blast straight through the center of everything Cesare had imagined he was.

"I had no idea love could be like this," he whispered, holding his precious child in his arms for the first time. He gazed down at his miracle of a wife. "But you did. You always did."

"It will only get better," she promised him.

And as with most things, Headmistress Higginbotham was right.

Over the years, they made seven more little creatures, each and every one of them messy and sticky and wild and feral—and absolutely perfect.

And at the end of those years of baby bellies, sleepless nights, and love so great it left them hollow with all that laughter, they sat out on his favorite terrace. They listened to Mattea lead the children in the musical revue that, by that point, people would pay to see her perform on stage, and smiled at each other.

They sat the way they had so long ago, Tuscany a gleaming bit of glory all around them. But all Cesare really needed was Beatrice. Even when he wasn't touching her, he could feel the things that held them together.

Like steel girders. Unbreakable and true.

The real legacy was this. Them. This passion that only deepened with time.

The family they'd made and the laughter they shared.

And the love he'd almost turned away, far brighter than any single candle in the darkness.

Because their love was molten gold, day after day and year after year, as bottomless as the sky and as dependable as the dawn.

And forever was a foregone conclusion. That was the only plan that mattered.

* * * * *

*Were you swept up in the drama of this
Caitlin Crews story?
Then check out her other fabulous books
for Presents!*

The Desert King's Kidnapped Virgin
The Spaniard's Last-Minute Wife
A Billion-Dollar Heir for Christmas
Wedding Night in the King's Bed
A Tycoon Too Wild to Wed

Available now!